This month, in **LONE STAR PRINCE**
by Cindy Gerard, meet Gregory Hunt—
a lawyer extraordinaire who hides his vulnerability
behind cynical eyes. Until he rescues the
one woman he could never forget,
Princess Anna von Oberland—a royal, regal beauty
whose son bears a striking resemblance to our hero!

**SILHOUETTE DESIRE
IS PROUD TO PRESENT THE**

**TEXAS
Cattleman's Club**

**Five wealthy Texas bachelors—all members of
the state's most exclusive club—set out on a
mission to rescue a princess...and find true love.**

* * *

We hope you've enjoyed the
exhilarating miniseries
Texas Cattleman's Club,
only from Silhouette Desire!

Dear Reader,

Merry Christmas from Silhouette Desire—where you're guaranteed powerful, passionate and provocative love stories that feature rugged heroes and spirited heroines who experience the full emotional intensity of falling in love!

The always-wonderful Cait London is back with this December's MAN OF THE MONTH, who happens to be one of THE BLAYLOCKS. In *Typical Male,* a modern warrior hero is attracted to the woman who wants to destroy him.

The thrilling Desire miniseries TEXAS CATTLEMAN'S CLUB concludes with *Lone Star Prince* by Cindy Gerard. Her Royal Princess Anna von Oberland finally reunites with the dashing attorney Gregory Hunt who fathered her child years ago.

Talented Ashley Summers returns to Desire with *That Loving Touch,* where a pregnant woman becomes snowbound with a sexy executive in his cabin. The ever-popular BACHELOR BATTALION gets into the holiday spirit with *Marine under the Mistletoe* by Maureen Child. *Star-Crossed Lovers* is a Romeo-and-Juliet-with-a-happy-ending story by Zena Valentine. And an honorable cowboy demands the woman pregnant with his child marry him in Christy Lockhart's *The Cowboy's Christmas Baby.*

Each and every month, Silhouette Desire offers you six exhilarating journeys into the seductive world of romance. So make a commitment to sensual love and treat yourself to all six for some great holiday reading this month!

Enjoy!

Joan Marlow Golan
Senior Editor, Silhouette Desire

Please address questions and book requests to:
Silhouette Reader Service
U.S.: 3010 Walden Ave., P.O. Box 1325, Buffalo, NY 14269
Canadian: P.O. Box 609, Fort Erie, Ont. L2A 5X3

Lone Star Prince
CINDY GERARD

Published by Silhouette Books
America's Publisher of Contemporary Romance

This book is dedicated to the ladies of the Club, Dixie Browning,
Caroline Cross, Peggy Moreland and Metsy Hingle.
Ladies—it's been a treat. I'm so glad I was along for the ride!
Special thanks to Leanne Banks, Susan Connell and
Glenna McReynolds for their friendship, their extraordinary insights
and their unflagging generosity. I love you guys.
Special thanks and acknowledgment are given to Cindy Gerard
for her contribution to the Texas Cattleman's Club series

 SILHOUETTE BOOKS

ISBN 0-373-76256-9

LONE STAR PRINCE

Copyright © 1999 by Harlequin Books S.A.

Visit us at www.romance.net

Printed in U.S.A.

Books by Cindy Gerard

Silhouette Desire

The Cowboy Takes a Lady #957
Lucas: The Loner #975
*The Bride Wore Blue #1012
*A Bride for Abel Greene #1052
*A Bride for Crimson Falls #1076
†The Outlaw's Wife #1175
†Marriage, Outlaw Style #1185
†The Outlaw Jesse James #1198
Lone Star Prince #1256

*Northern Lights Brides
†Outlaw Hearts

CINDY GERARD

If asked "What's your idea of heaven?" Cindy Gerard would say a warm sun, a cool breeze, pan pizza and a good book. If she had to settle for one of the four, she'd opt for the book, with the pizza running a close second. Inspired by the pleasure she's received from the books she's read and her longtime love affair with her husband, Tom, Cindy now creates her own warm, evocative stories about compelling characters and complex relationships.

All that reading must have paid off, because since winning the Waldenbooks Award for Best Selling Series Romance for a First-Time Author, Cindy has gone on to win the prestigious Colorado Romance Writers' Award of Excellence, *Romantic Times Magazine* W.I.S.H. awards, Career Achievement and Reviewers' Choice nominations and the Romance Writers of America's RITA Award nomination for Best Short Contemporary Romance.

"What's Happening in Royal?"

NEWS FLASH, December 1999—Rumors are running rampant about town that an actual royal princess may be in our midst! There have been unconfirmed reports that Princess Anna von Oberland is missing from her European country of Obersbourg, and may be hiding out in our own Royal, TX. Imagine...a princess in Royal—who would've "thunk" it?

Could our rugged *Texas Cattleman's Club* members know the whereabouts of Her Royal Highness?

There are those who say that Gregory Hunt— hotshot attorney, Cattleman's Club member and most eligible of bachelors—may have more than a passing interest in the lovely Princess Anna. In fact, rumor has it that they shared a passionate tryst years ago in her far-off land....

Will the princess be discovered here... and rumors be put to rest? Please stay tuned!

Prologue

September 5th, 2:00 a.m.
Somewhere over the Atlantic

Hollywood couldn't have staged a more dicey plot. An evil prince. A beautiful princess in his clutches. A midnight rescue by an ex-marine and ex-lover, charging in to save the day.

Trouble was, this wasn't Hollywood. It was all too real, and as Greg Hunt stared grimly across the cabin of the private jet bound for the States, he hadn't yet decided if he was the hero or the chump in this little melodrama.

The woman gazing vacantly out the window of the starboard side of the aircraft was exhausted, but still, her bearing was regal, her posture erect.

Four years ago when Greg had first met her she'd been beautiful. There was no denying, she was beautiful still.

Yet Princess Anna von Oberland, loved by the paparazzi, adored by the masses, had been robbed of the wide-eyed innocence that had struck him as both intriguing and irresistible those many years ago. A haunted, hunted edge had painted pale violet smudges beneath her summer-green eyes, drawn fine lines of tension around a smile that was forced and shallow and reserved only for the child sleeping at her side. Her silk and velvet voice, with its honeyed, husky resonance, spoke of lost summers and faded dreams and hinted of her European lineage only when she was exhausted. Like now.

Shifting uneasily, Greg took his own turn staring out the window into the blackness of night at thirty-one thousand feet. He tried to divorce himself from an unrelenting need to hold her. Seeing her like this—seeing her again—had brought back feelings he'd thought were dead and buried. And while he was relieved she had turned to him for help—was prepared to do whatever it took to protect her—he was also determined not to let her or her solemn-eyed little boy breach the wall he'd built around his emotions when she'd walked away from him four years ago.

Determined, but unfortunately, not one hundred percent successful, he admitted grudgingly. Against all resolve, his mind wandered back to the summer night they'd first met. He'd been a marine on his last tour of duty and then had to return to Texas to take his place as heir apparent to the Hunt dynasty. On leave in the little European principality of Obersbourg, he'd been taken in completely by the guileless little peasant girl whose eyes had been only for him. He hadn't known she'd been a princess on the run from her family, her obligations and the stark reality of her position in life—

just as she hadn't known he was anything but a lowly marine.

It seemed like a lifetime ago that their eyes had met, locked, held across a street full of dancers in the plaza. A lifetime since they'd woven their way unerringly through the crowd and into each other's arms. Since they'd danced. Fallen in love. Made love. And when her true identity had come out, they parted.

He quickly checked the memory. There was no point hashing over that again. It had been four years. He'd put it all behind him—at least he had until he'd received her transatlantic call last week and the panicked sound of her voice had brought it all back like it was yesterday.

"Gregory. I need you. Please come. Please…come."

So he had. With the backing of Texas billionaire Hank Langley—and Langley's Avenger, a Hunt Industries aircraft—the able assistance of Sterling Churchill and Forrest Cunningham, all members of Langley's Texas Cattleman's Club, they'd smuggled the princess and her son out from under the Obersbourg royal guard not three hours ago. All ex-military men, they had created the Alpha team to tackle this mission.

He scrubbed the back of his knuckles absently against the stubble on his jaw and stared broodily into the dark. As corporate counsel for Hunt Industries and CEO of several companies under the Hunt umbrella, he'd had plenty of work to keep him busy. So he was damned if he knew why he'd been so ready to let himself get wrapped up in her life again. He only knew that this time, it wasn't by chance. This time there was more at stake than reckless hearts and stolen moments. He didn't have all the details sorted out, but he knew that Anna's sister, Sara, and Sara's lover were dead, the victims of a mysterious car crash. Sara's infant twins were in the physical custody of Ivan Striksky, the playboy prince of Asterland, who was holding them the equivalent of political hostages as part of a plot to force Anna to marry him. And Greg, it seemed, had been cast in the role of white knight.

White knight, hell, he thought as the hushed whispers of Churchill and Cunningham—men he'd been glad to have guarding his back—drifted from the aft end of the Avenger. This little caper had international incident written all over it. It was going to take a damn sight more than his law degree to smooth some very ruffled, very royal European feathers when this thing broke wide open and the King and Queen of Obersbourg discovered their golden goose was missing.

He stretched his long legs out in front of him, figuring he'd deal with it when it happened. In the meantime, the only part he had left to play in this little scenario was to see Anna safely to the States. She was a resourceful woman; she'd figure out where to go from there. All he needed to do was get on with his life—and quit thinking about why this woman, above all women, could mess up his head in more ways than he could catalog or name.

William stirred in his sleep. Making a protective shield of her body, Anna folded him closer to her side. Her reaction was instinctive though, at the moment, unnecessary. There was no threat here. Not in this jet with Gregory. At least there was no physical threat. Uncertainty, however, was still an ugly reality. For her it was too real and too chilling even though, for the time being, they were safe from Ivan. And they were free from her parents, who had been willing to sacrifice her and, ultimately, William to Ivan in exchange for a financial bailout to save Obersbourg's sovereignty.

William cried out, startling her out of her thoughts. His small voice was a panicked, frightened mew in the humming silence of the pressurized cabin.

"Shh, baby. Momma's here." Small for his age, William was often mistaken for a year younger than the precious age of four he would turn on his next birthday. She scooped him onto her lap, cradled his face to her breast, murmured in soothing tones. "It's okay. Momma's here."

She pressed her lips to the top of his head, then laid her cheek there as he drifted back to sleep.

"Is he okay?" Gregory's deep voice was a soft rumble of concern.

She nodded, wanting to assure him as much as herself. Enfolding William in security and warmth, she gained her own small measure of comfort from the solid pressure of his little compact body snuggled against her. "He's fine. This has all just been a little frightening for him."

Although he held his silence, Anna could feel Gregory's dark gaze on her, then on William. She could sense the questions she knew he would ask. And she prayed for the answers that would satisfy him, asked forgiveness for the lies her lack of courage would force her to tell.

"Where's his father, Anna? Why was it me you called and not him?"

His question was sharp and direct, fitting since this was the moment that had been looming in the shadows of all else that had happened. She'd been bracing for it, had carefully concocted the lie, woven it ruthlessly around the truth.

"He's never been a part of William's life," she said, then slowed her words, shook off the accent only her nerves and fatigue had allowed to slip into her speech.

"What his father and I shared..." Purposefully, she let the thought trail off, gave a small shrug, an invitation for him to draw his own conclusions. "I...I had hoped for more."

"He abandoned you?" A swift, dangerous anger underscored each word.

"No," she said quickly. "Oh, no. Not abandoned. Let's...let's just leave it at it wasn't meant to be."

In the darkness, she sensed Gregory's gaze drift over William, studying his dark brown hair, his slight little frame, picturing, perhaps, his Mediterranean-blue eyes.

"I'm so sorry to have involved you in this, Gregory," she said abruptly, speared by a piercing need to steer the attention away from William. "I...I didn't know where else to turn."

"I told you..." His voice was soft, even if his eyes were hard. "I told you that if you ever needed me I'd be there for you."

Yes. Yes, he had told her, and even four years later, she'd known she could count on him. After all, it was his strength that had drawn her to him in the beginning—his strength and his earthy, middle class charm. At least she'd thought then that he was just a working man. It wasn't until last year that she'd seen an article on Hunt Industries and realized that Gregory was the equivalent of American royalty. The irony was so very hard to accept.

She'd been feeling the burden of her position, of centuries of tradition, of familial obligations that fateful summer. In one of her rare acts of rebellion, she'd disguised herself as a village girl and escaped it all for a few hours to get lost in the fantasy atmosphere of the summer street festival—and ended up spending four glorious days and nights with Gregory. She'd given in completely to her instant and overpowering love for the exciting, fun-loving American who not only showed her a glimpse of a freedom she'd never known but also introduced her to true passion and the one great love of her life.

He'd been so...so American. Strong. Vital. So guilelessly arrogant in his self-confidence, utterly charming for his lack of pretense. And so beautiful. In his close-cropped military haircut, his crisply creased olive drabs that hugged his rugged body and showcased the breadth and the depth of the man within, he'd made her fall fast and hard. Though he could never know it, she'd also fallen forever.

A vivid memory of the day they parted hit her with a startling sense of presence. She remembered every pulse beat of that day, recalled with a sharp twist to her heart the moment she'd told him the truth about who she was, and why they couldn't be together. Angry, he'd scribbled his phone number across an American dollar bill and pressed it into her hand. His blue eyes had been stormy, his jaw set in anger and pride. *"If you ever need anything, call this number."*

In the diluted cabin light, she searched his eyes for any sign of the passion that had flared between them then. She saw only a sense of duty, a cold stare of indifference. Yet he had kept his promise. He had come for her. Tears stung her eyes, tightened her throat. If only someone could have been there to save Sara.

Sara was dead and now the twins were lost to Anna, too.

"Sara's babies," she murmured, suddenly overwhelmed by feelings of helplessness and cowardice, her fear for them equaled only by her sense of failure. "I shouldn't have left without them."

"Anna...there was no way we could get them out this trip. We cut it too close as it was. I promise you, the Alpha team made plans for my brother, Blake, to rescue them."

She blinked back the moisture matting her lashes, knowing she was weak for wanting to believe him. Just as he was strong—as she'd known only he could be strong.

"You trusted me to come for you." His tone forced her to focus on him, on now. When she did, his eyes restated his words as a question that demanded an answer.

She nodded. *Yes. She had trusted him.*

"Then trust me one more time. Blake will find them. He'll bring them to you."

Clinging to the strength of his conviction, she let her head drop back against the headrest, made herself draw a calming breath. Distancing herself from her fear for the babies, she smoothed a tuft of downy fine hair from William's brow. "You never bargained for this. And I never dreamed I'd have to call on you someday. How can I ever thank you?"

"Level with me," he said, point-blank, and her heart skipped several beats. "Tell me everything...everything so I can help get you out of this mess."

Everything. She turned her head away. He deserved to know everything. She couldn't give him what he deserved. Not now. She enfolded William closer to her side. Maybe not ever. But he was right. If she was going to survive this, if she was to escape Ivan's far-reaching power and undermine his plans, she had to tell him something. Enough, at least, to keep William safe and keep her from becoming Ivan's wife and political pawn for the rest of her life.

Aware suddenly that Gregory was speaking to her again, she turned to him, tried to clear her head.

"Why don't you rest, Anna." He offered the suggestion with a gentleness that was almost her undoing, as if he sensed she simply couldn't handle anymore tonight. "You're exhausted. Try to get some sleep. We'll sort this all out after we land and get the two of you settled."

She was too relieved with the reprieve to do anything but thank him again. And to ask the inevitable question.

"Where are we going?"

For the first time since he'd stolen her and William from their quarters in the west wing of Obersbourg Palace, he smiled. "Why, we're going home, sugar." A very slow, very deliberate western drawl had slipped into his voice like warm honey. "My home. West Texas."

Texas. Arid plains, wide open spaces. Cowboys. She remembered his words from that summer when he'd talked about his home with such pride. *Miles and miles of nothing but sky. And oil wells. Lots of oil wells.*

It sounded like a good place to hide. It sounded like a good place to heal. Carefully, she offered her own smile. "I've always wanted to see a cowboy."

His eyes softened a fraction. "Well that works out just fine then, because I reckon there're a few cowboys who will be pleased as punch to see you, too."

While his words were meant to lighten the mood and ease her tension, they had the opposite effect.

"Don't worry, Anna."

She met his eyes. Saw again that he had sensed her concern.

"No one in town will know who you are, much less recognize you. We've seen to that."

He seemed both satisfied and sure—and, unaccountably, amused by a prospect he chose not to share with her.

That was fair, she decided. She had her secret. She'd let him have his. For now it was enough to know she was free of Ivan. At least for the moment. And the moment was what she needed most.

It wasn't over. It might never be over. But she had breathing room now. And she had time. Time to regroup, to assess, to think of a way to save her country without sacrificing her son and herself in the process. Until she accomplished that, she had to believe in Gregory to keep her safe and bring her Sara's babies.

Exhausted, she finally let the fatigue overtake her. With William safe for the moment and snug by her side, she let her eyes drift close, let months of tension ease from her body and finally gave in to the haven of sleep.

Greg sensed the moment the nervous energy that had fueled Anna hit empty. In the darkness he watched her drift into an embracing sleep. He still didn't know what had prompted her to turn to him. Couldn't entertain even a guess—or didn't want to—because all the explanations started with that long ago summer and ended with the wanting to pick up where they'd left off. The one thing he was sure of in all of this mess was that he couldn't let that happen. He was wiser now and he'd be damned if he'd let her break through his defenses again.

Yet he couldn't stop himself from taking stock of her classic beauty as she slept—the porcelain complexion, long blond hair, gently winged brows, wide-set eyes, regally sculpted cheekbones—and feel a hard knot of yearning tighten in his gut. He checked it as abruptly as it started. Obviously, she hadn't lost sleep over their parting. The child at her side was the proof of that. More to the point, it drove home one indisputable fact: she hadn't wasted any time moving from his bed to another.

A part of him would like to hate her for that. He didn't have it in him. Just like he didn't have it in him to love her. Not again. Not even in the face of the danger she was in. Not even in the face of the temptation.

He looked away. *For the last time, there was no reason to go there.* She was as out of bounds now as she'd been then. Only now, he was wise enough to know up front where the boundaries began. More importantly, he knew where they ended. And he no longer needed her to spell it out for him. She, after all, was a princess. And as she'd so convincingly implied four years ago, he was no prince.

What he was, he acknowledged with a grim set to his mouth, was a sucker for a damsel in distress. What he would be, he assured himself as he looked away from the tumble of blond hair framing her face, was damn glad when this blew over and Her Royal Highness jet-setted out of his life again and got back to the one she'd been born and bred to live.

One

Four months later. The Royal Diner, Royal, Texas

Gearing up for the breakfast rush, Anna snagged a juice glass on her way to the cooler, filled it and breezed on out toward booth number six. She reset the coffeemaker on her way by as a fleeting thought of her wild escape from Obersbourg four months ago ran through her mind. So much had happened—the risky rescue, the safety factor that was at best a fluid thing while Ivan continued a full-scale search for her, her fear for Sara's babies until Gregory's brother, Blake, had rescued them and brought them safely to Royal. Yet in spite of all that, a soft smile tilted her lips as she thought of something Gregory had said to her on that midnight flight. Something that had seemed ominous then, amusing now.

"Don't worry, Anna. No one in town will know who you are, much less recognize you. We've seen to that."

At the time, she hadn't understood what he'd meant. Two days later he'd shown up at her door with a pink polyester uniform and instructed her to report for work as a waitress at the Royal Diner as part of her cover to keep her identity concealed. She'd understood perfectly then.

As unthinkable as it had seemed at the time, his intent had been as clear as Waterford crystal: Anna von Oberland—whose royal blood lines could be traced back over seven centuries, who had been tutored by the most prestigious private instructors in Europe, then Swiss educated at the collegiate level, who owned advanced degrees in business and economics, who was successor to the throne of kings—was to be transformed from Her Most Serene Royal Highness, the Esteemed Princess of Obersbourg, to a waitress, in the form of down-home girl, Annie Grace.

The unthinkable hadn't ended there. Neither had the surprises. In the past months since she'd been hiding out in Royal as Annie Grace, she'd not only played the part of Annie Grace, she'd been having the time of her life.

One of the reasons for all that fun grinned at her from behind the grill as she elbowed up to the cook's counter to place an order.

A pair of coal-black eyes met hers, sparkling flirtatiously. "You have a need, Annie-mine?"

"I have a need for a short stack, two eggs over easy, a side of bacon, wheat-no-butter, please, Manny."

"Sure thing, Annie sweetheart, darlin' dear. Anything else I can do for you while my fire's hot?"

Anna tried unsuccessfully to hide a smile. Even if she hadn't caught the meaningful waggle of Manny Reno's dark brows, she'd have known he wasn't referring to the fire under his grill. Manny, a beautiful Chicano bodybuilder and part-time cook, was an incorrigible and accomplished flirt. And like most of the hardy Texans she'd met since Gregory had eased her quietly into Royal four months ago, he was also about as dangerous as a slice of his coconut cream pie.

Grinning, she clipped the order to the revolving wheel above the counter and reached for the coffeepot. "Give me a break, Manny. It's 6:00 a.m. It's Monday. I haven't built up the strength yet to spar with you."

"Well, you see now, beautiful girl…" Manny's black eyes danced from the rich caramel backdrop of his face. "…that's all part of my strategy. Get'cha while you're not awake enough to fight this intense attraction you feel for me."

"Well…there is that." She shot him a coy smile then sobered abruptly. "Oh, wait." Bracing a hand to her forehead, she closed her eyes. "I feel something—yes. Here it is now. My better judgment just arrived to save the day. Whew. That was close. For a minute there, I almost lost my head. Sorry, Manny—and we were going to have such a good time, too."

"Oh, maaan." Manny groaned, heavy on the theatrics, as he poured batter onto the griddle, then expertly flipped an omelette. "You are breaking my heart here."

Sheila Foster sidled up to the counter just then, hooked an order on the clip. She sliced Anna a quick, conspiratorial wink before firing her own shot at Manny. "You gotta have a heart to get one broken."

Sheila was currently single, twice divorced and fighting a size twelve for all she was worth. The fact that she had a hard and heavy case on Manny wasn't lost on Anna. Neither was it lost on Manny, who, after almost two months of drooling over Sheila, hadn't worked up the courage to do something about it.

"Who's callin' the kettle black, little Sheba?" Manny accused with a grin so sweet Anna could almost taste the honey.

"It's Sheila, you big ape, and I've got a heart. I just don't see any point wasting any extra beats over you."

"You know you're nuts about me, my little chili pepper."

"The only one nuts around here is you. Now is my number five up yet or did you have to run down a chicken and squeeze the eggs out of her?"

Laughing at their good-natured sniping, Anna headed for the booth where Homer Gaffney sat. Homer smiled when she approached, causing deep creases to dig even deeper grooves into the wizened old face that looked up at her from beneath the dusty brim of a stained and dented straw cowboy hat.

"Here's your juice, Homer. And you're drinking regular, not decaf this morning, right?"

"Gotta have the high octane this mornin', Annie. Full day ahead a' me. Movin' the herd. From the sound of things we'll be bucking stout sou'west winds and a boatload of dust. I'm gonna need all the caffeine I can get."

As she filled Homer's cup, she felt that little prickle of unease that sometimes crept up on her when someone looked at her in that I've-seen-you-before-kind-of-way. The way Homer was looking at her now.

"I just can't get over how much you look like that fancy princess woman. Oh, what is her name, anyway?"

"Fergie?" she suggested and worked hard at manufacturing a teasing smile.

"Naw. That other one—the one from some foreign sounding place. You sure you ain't some long lost twin got switched at birth?"

"Homer, Homer." She forced a playful, chiding tone.

"Last week you said you thought I looked like a movie star. I'll tell you what, though—if you can figure out some way to make me into a princess, I'll figure out a way to make you my prince."

Homer laughed, blushed and tugged on his hat brim. "I'd be more frog than prince—and I don't allow my Martha would much go for me running off with you. It's a nice thought, though, huh?"

"You bet, Homer." She laid a hand on his shoulder then walked away. "It's a very nice thought."

It was also a thought that, thankfully, didn't occur too often. When it did, she generally handled it the same way as she had with Homer just now. She'd laugh, joke and walk away. So far it had worked. Yet the possibility always loomed that the day might come when her luck on that count would run out and someone would recognize her.

Refusing to think about that now, she answered Manny's ding—he signaled with a little silver bell when an order was up—and delivered an omelette and a sweet roll. Then she quickly bussed two tables and raked in two dollars and some odd change in tips. As she headed back for Homer's short stack and eggs, she was completely oblivious of the diner's shortcomings when compared to the grandeur that had once been her life at Obersbourg Palace.

The Royal Diner was your basic greasy spoon café, nonalcoholic watering hole, town meeting place and coffee klatch all wrapped up in one. Just as unlikely as Anna becoming adept as a waitress was the fact that the diner had also become her refuge. She loved every inch of the place—from the worn and cracked dull-gray linoleum floor tiles to the faded red plastic on the booth seats to the scratched chrome strips edging the tabletops and the counter with its dozen stools.

She loved the steamy warmth of it. The smell of it. The sinfully juicy hamburgers that Manny cooked on his grill, the decadently thick chocolate malts that she had learned to make on the ancient malt machine. She even loved the thin film of smoke and grease coating the plate glass windows that Hazel, the owner, had tried to pretty up with muslin curtains.

She knew it wasn't supposed to work like this. She knew that Gregory had set her up with this waitress ruse because he thought she would consider it menial and beneath her. A princess wasn't supposed to mingle with, let alone wait on, the common folk. It was his subtle way, she supposed, of paying her back for what she'd done to him years ago.

She understood his motives. She even forgave him. Just like she forgave him for making himself as scarce as a snowstorm in West Texas. Even though his deliberate absence hurt, she figured he was entitled. He'd known she would be forced to take the waitress job—as he'd put it, hiding in plain sight—rather than risk having undue attention focused on the reclusive young woman and child in The Royal Court Complex, apartment 3B.

What Gregory hadn't understood was that while she had been apprehensive at first, it was because she had been afraid she couldn't do the work, not because she didn't want to do it. Another thing Gregory hadn't understood was that while normal little girls dreamed of castles, servants and knights in shining armor, Anna had dreamed of walking barefoot in the grass, of playing hide-and-seek after dark with the village children, of a best friend to share secrets with.

What she had always wanted was to be a part of something as an equal, not set apart as elite. As Princess Anna von Oberland, she'd done elite. She'd lived elite. Elite was lonely and isolating. She'd lived lavishly, surrounded by rare artwork, gilded mirrors and armies of servants. She'd slept in platform beds beneath satin sheets. And yet everything she'd ever wanted had been out of her reach: the ultimate excitement of the absolutely mundane.

As Annie Grace, the waitress, she'd found that—in an austere two-bedroom apartment and, of all things, an alarm clock. She loved her alarm clock. Like William, it gave her purpose. It gave her a reason to get up and be useful on the most basic level.

Here, in Royal, she was a small part of a whole, and despite everything that had happened, it felt wonderful. She was a single mom, working for a living. And she felt, for the first time in her life, as if she belonged. It was another of life's strange ironies that as she played the role of a waitress, she felt more real than at any other time in her life.

Even better, since arriving in Royal, she was seeing things in William that she had always yearned to see. While he was still reserved and slow to trust, he smiled more. He even laughed sometimes without fear of reprisal. Harriet Sherman, her next door neighbor and volunteer baby-sitter, had been responsible for much of that.

Manny hit the bell again, snapping her head up. She hurried to pick up a morning special and remembered how difficult it had been to leave William in Harriet's care that first morning. Even with Gregory's assurances that Harriet was his employee and that he'd positioned her next door to Anna's apartment for the sole purpose of looking after both her and William, it had been hard leaving him.

Now it was hard to think of taking him away from here, away from Harriet and her loving arms and oatmeal raisin cookies. But she knew she must eventually return to Obersbourg and face her obligations.

She squared her shoulders, drew a bracing breath. Ivan wouldn't call off his dogs. He would not give up on trying to strong-arm her into marriage. And as much as it hurt to acknowledge it, her parents would continue to offer her up to Ivan as the prize to save Obersbourg's sovereignty.

Even accepting all this, she knew she must return. Obersbourg was her country. Her birthright. Her obligation. Hopefully, she would be stronger for her time here in Royal. Hopefully, she would come up with a solution to her country's grave dilemma that didn't require marriage to a man she had despised even before she'd begun to suspect he was involved in Sara's death.

For all of those reasons, the thought of leaving Royal haunted her. Soon, though, she would have one less reason to stay. As of Sunday, her final tie to her sister, Sara, would be severed. One more link with Ivan would be broken. And while Gregory would never be hers again to lose, one more reason for his protection would also be negated.

Her sunny mood of moments ago was as lost as the sun that had disappeared beneath the dust inspired by a tenacious and sustained wind. Reality encroached severely on Annie Grace's fantasy world. Like an unyielding and vengeful enemy, it deposited the weight of obligation and the cold hard facts of duty back into the hands of Anna von Oberland—all to the relentless tick of the clock as time slowly ran out on her.

The King and Queen of Obersbourg's entire existence exemplified saving face at all costs, celebrated the triumph of appearance over reality. So it was sadly ironic, Anna thought, that in her boldest act of defiance yet, she had resorted to practicing the ruling principle of her parents' lives—a principle she abhorred.

This Sunday, however, she played their game to the letter. She watched the happy celebration unfold before her in the grand salon of the Texas Cattleman's Club with a plastic smile in place when the reality was that her heart was breaking. She murmured the appropriate words when her only triumph was in the knowledge that no one knew how much her actions had cost her.

As promised, Miranda and Edward, her sister's twin babies, had been rescued by Gregory's brother Blake. They were safe—thank God they were safe here in Texas—but as of today, they were no longer hers to protect. As of today, they were no longer hers at all.

In one of the hardest decisions of her life, she had given them up. She had given them over to the loving arms of Blake and his new bride, Josie.

It was the right thing to do, she told herself, just as she had told herself repeatedly since Blake had brought the babies to Texas. Blake and Josie loved them. They would ensure that Anna's promise to Sara would be fulfilled.

"Promise me, Anna. Promise me," Sara had pleaded shortly after the twins were born. *"If anything happens to me...promise me you won't let mother and father raise them. Promise me you'll get them out of Obersbourg and find someone who will love and nurture them."*

Anna had smiled back then at her little sister's dramatic plea. Sara had always been the actress of the two of them. The rebel. The wild little princess who thumbed her nose in the face of tradition, laughed at the rigors of royal protocol.

Bracing against a fresh wave of pain, Anna drew herself erect. It was because of Ivan Striksky that Sara would never laugh again. The final proof had arrived yesterday. Gregory had sent the damning evidence over to the diner via messenger.

She was still trying to come to grips with the words in the fax sent by the attorney who had handled the estate of Marcus Dumond, Ivan's horse trainer. Marcus had been much more than a horse trainer, as it turned out. Anna had known he had once been Sara's lover. She hadn't known that Marcus was the father of the twins. And now, because Gregory had ferreted out the truth, she had proof that the car crash that had killed both Sara and Marcus had been arranged by Ivan.

The rumble of deep, masculine laughter dragged her away from her thoughts of that devastating news and back to the reason for today's celebration. Today was the day she had agreed to officially release the twins for adoption. Today was the day she severed her last tie to Sara.

She made herself shut out the ugly string of events that had brought her here and focused on the happiness around her. Blake was a good man. Josie a good woman. Both were all smiles as they stood side by side, each of them cradling one of the babies in their arms. And while she had agonized about her decision, in the end she knew she'd had no choice. It had been Sara's wish.

Just like she'd had no choice but to attend today's celebration. Thank God for Harriet, she thought, as she so often had in the past months. Sensing intuitively that Anna would need to draw on all her resources to keep herself together, she had volunteered to take William to a movie today.

"Anna?"

She blinked, automatically set a smile in place even before she realized it was Josie who had walked up beside her and lightly touched her arm.

"Are you all right?"

"Fine. I'm fine." She broadened her smile, and even though her heart was breaking, opened her arms to little Miranda when Josie held her out to her. Tears filled her eyes as Miranda reached up and tangled her little fingers in Anna's hair.

Life was so strange, she thought, smiling down at the happily gurgling baby. When Blake had finally managed to smuggle the babies out of Europe and into Texas, he'd run into the storm of the century while driving across the state with them. Josie had spotted his car in a washed-out ravine. Blake had been unconscious, the babies crying and hungry. Josie had managed to get them all home to her farmhouse, and during Blake's recovery, while he'd struggled to regain his memory that had been temporarily lost in the crash, they'd fallen deeply in love—with each other and with the twins.

"She's beautiful, isn't she?" Josie murmured, breaking into Anna's thoughts.

"Yes," Anna agreed softly. Relishing the warmth and the sweet scent of the baby in her arms, she held her closer. "She's very beautiful."

The silence that followed rang hollow with the unspoken pain of her loss.

"You will always be her aunt, Anna." Sensitive to Anna's regrets, Josie's eyes, when Anna met them, were kind and reassuring. "You will always be Edward's aunt. They're your family. Please, don't doubt that. We won't ever take that away from you.''

Anna blinked hard, gave Josie a genuine smile as Blake, with Edward sleeping soundly in his arms, joined them.

''I know,'' she said. ''Just like I know they'll have a far better home and life with you than if I were to take them back to Obersbourg.''

She didn't doubt that for one moment. Even as William's mother, she had difficulty exercising authority over how he was raised. As the twins' aunt, her influence would be even more limited. She couldn't bear to have happen to them what happened to Sara. She couldn't let two sweet, precious lives be ruled by the iron fist of her father and the apathetic blind eye of her mother. If subjected to her parents' strict code of discipline, like Sara, they might eventually rebel. Like Sara, they might turn to a wild and destructive lifestyle—like the one that had played a part in ending her life.

Her next words were spoken as much to herself as to Blake and Josie. ''They have a chance for a normal life now. I have to believe that.'' She stopped, braced and deliberately met Josie's concerned gaze, then Blake's. ''I *do* believe that. Just like I believe Sara would have approved. You're very special. Both of you.''

Blake's warm brown eyes, so different from his brother Gregory's distant blue, probed hers. ''No regrets?''

She kissed Miranda lightly on the cheek and handed her back to Josie before answering with conviction. ''I have many regrets in all of this—the decision to give up the twins to you is not one of them.''

Josie embraced her then, her own eyes brimming with tears.

"Oh, no." Anna managed a shaky laugh. "Don't you dare start. I'm lost if you cry—and this is a party, remember? Go. Go party."

"You're okay then?" Blake touched a hand to her arm.

"I told you. I'm fine. Now go. I saw your father looking for you."

As she watched them walk away, a bittersweet ache in her chest, someone accidentally bumped into her, then apologized profusely. For the first time today, her smile was spontaneous. Since Gregory had brought her here to Royal, she had grown to appreciate the Texas style of gallantry, the open friendliness of its people.

She made herself focus on the gathering, recognized many of the faces, faces of people who knew her as Annie Grace, just a waitress at the diner. Aside from Blake and Josie, only Gregory and Harriet and the three men who had assisted him on the Alpha mission to rescue her last September—Hank Langley, Sterling Churchill, Forrest Cunningham—knew her true identity. They too, had joined the celebration. So had their wives, Callie, Susan, and Becky.

She had taken special notice of Gregory and Blake's parents, Janine and Carson Hunt. She wasn't certain how much Gregory's parents knew about the twins' situation—or about hers. She only knew that they looked at her through kind eyes that made her yearn for something she'd never received from her own parents. Carson was a robust bear of a man with crinkled brown eyes and a thick head of silver hair. Janine was lovely. Diminutive in stature, yet obviously her own woman, her blue eyes, so like Gregory's, were warm, bold and full of life as she welcomed Edward and Miranda to the family with loving arms.

The only person noticeably absent was Gregory. True to form, since that September morning when he'd settled her into the apartment, he had made it a point to be absent if she was anywhere in the vicinity. His influence had been known in many other ways, however. It was Gregory who had expedited the adoption process by calling in some markers, taking advantage of his connections with both the bar and the bench. And it was the respect he'd earned in the community that had kept public speculation about the twins' parentage to a minimum. There was acceptance that they now belonged to Blake and Josie—a simple fact.

It was for the best all around that he maintained his distance from her, she knew. It saved her from answering questions for which he would eventually demand answers. Still, there was regret associated with the knowledge. Just as there was a sudden, chest-tightening anticipation when, on the heels of those thoughts, Gregory walked in the door.

Her heart clenched, as it always did, when she saw him. His dark good looks and impressive presence set him apart even in this room full of men who were unequaled among men. Above all else, though, the tension strung tight around his mouth, the intensity in his eyes held her riveted as he walked unerringly toward her.

When he took her hand in his, relayed the need for silence through a quick, firm squeeze, she was filled with a sudden, intuitive awareness that what he was about to tell her would change her life forever.

Her heart skipped several beats. "Gregory…what is it?"

She searched his face with a heightening premonition of dread as he shook his head then sought and found his brother and the men who had been in on the Alpha rescue mission. With a clipped lift of his chin, he signaled them to follow him.

Her heart plummeted to her stomach as he led her in suspended silence to a small room off the main salon. Langley, Churchill, and Sterling, along with Blake and Josie, who had handed off the twins to Gregory's parents, followed then shut the door behind them.

"What's happened?" Panic had become a valid and violent contender for the apprehension that clogged her throat.

After a moment's pause, Gregory captured her gaze with the same strength as his firm grip on her hands.

"Ivan Striksky is dead." The softness of his voice was no cushion for the shock of his announcement.

The jolt weakened her knees. With Gregory's solemn arrival, she'd expected news of Ivan. But this...

She felt suddenly as if she'd fallen into a vacuous tunnel, where sound, shape and texture blended together in a numbing, surreal kaleidoscope of confusion.

"Dead?" she heard someone ask and knew on a peripheral level that someone was her.

A circle of concerned faces closed supportively around her. She heard Josie's soft voice whisper her name and urge her to sit down as Hank settled a protective hand to her back.

"What...how?"

A hush filled the room as the four men and one woman who were privileged to the specifics of Anna's true identity and her midnight flight from Obersbourg listened in stunned amazement as Gregory related what details he had managed to find out about Prince Ivan Striksky's suicide.

Two

She was running…running through maze after maze. Long bony hands grabbed at her. Chased unrelentingly. She was so tired. Her legs wouldn't support her. She stumbled, searched, desperate to find a light that never came. For a haven that never opened to her. Then she was trapped. And the hands. Hundreds of hands grabbed at her…

Heart racing, Anna bolted wildly up in bed, wrestled with tangled sheets. Stumbling blindly to the window, she threw it open, swallowing a scream. Even in the grips of the nightmare, her concern was for William. She didn't want to frighten him. He'd been through enough.

A reassuring rush of arid, West Texas air hit her full in the face as she braced her palms on the sill. She dragged it in—deep, hungry drafts—and willed herself toward lucidity.

Clinging desperately to the reality that was now, she reached for the presence of mind that would assure her it was over. They were safe.

Even after months of haunting her nights, when the nightmare hit, it still took Anna by surprise. Tonight it was worse than the other nights. Tonight it had grabbed her by the throat. Had her heart slamming in her chest, her breath catching. The hideous grip of it had strangled her as darkness enfolded her in cloying, suffocating isolation.

Calmer now, she opened her eyes, felt a cool breeze feather across her perspiration-drenched skin and sagged in weary relief against the open window frame. Then she made herself recount the last four months in her mind to cement the fact one more time that it was really over.

She and William were safe.

The twins were safe with Blake and Josie.

And Ivan was dead.

Ivan was dead.

She shivered and drew away from the window as the memory of his suicide and the December breeze rustling her damp nightgown combined to pebble her skin with gooseflesh. Dragging a hand through her tousled hair, she sank back down on the edge of the bed, dug her palms into the blanket at her hips and forced several steadying breaths.

It was at times like these that she wished she could drink like some of the rowdy Texans she'd grown to know and appreciate since she'd arrived in Royal. A good, stiff shot of straight-up bourbon might settle the demons that had robbed her of yet another night's sleep.

''Face them,'' she whispered into the darkness.

There is no more fear, she reminded herself staunchly

and willed the residual trembling in her hands to steady. *No more fear.* Only decisions that needed to be made. So many decisions—

A sudden pounding on her door shot her heart straight back to her throat. She vaulted to her feet, whirled toward the sound.

"Anna...Anna are you all right?"

Gregory.

Relief was swift and draining as she rushed toward the door, not wanting to wake William who was sound asleep in the other bedroom. When she reached the small foyer, she threw the deadbolt. With both hands clutching the heavy steel door, she opened it a crack and met the dark concern in a pair of hard blue eyes shaded by the brim of a coal-black Stetson.

Since those first few days when Gregory had settled her into this small apartment, he had never again crossed the threshold. The cool message of that statement had not been lost to her. He had come to her aid when she'd needed him, but he'd made it clear as a Texas sky that he wanted no part of her life. So seeing him here now, at this hour, on the heels of the nightmare, was beyond her comprehension.

"What...what are you doing here?"

His expression was as dark as the night, his eyes as cool as chipped ice. "I was on my way home from the Club when the lights on the alarm panel in my pickup lit up like a Christmas tree."

She sagged against the door, raked the hair away from her face as understanding dawned. When he'd first shown her the apartment, he'd told her with terse words and military precision about the silent alarm he'd installed on all the windows and doors in the event Ivan found her. The alarm was electronically linked to the Texas Cattleman's Club that he and the rest of the Alpha team frequented to his home in Pine Valley and his personal vehicles.

"I didn't think. I...I had a bad dream," she confessed with reluctance. "I needed some air and threw open the window. I'm sorry. I forgot about the alarm system."

Greg stared down at the woman who had created enough havoc in his life to mount a small uprising. He'd known when he'd answered her call for help last August that he'd been opening up a Pandora's box full of problems. He'd been prepared for the investment of time, tactics and diplomacy. He'd had to employ plenty of both, not the least of which had been keeping Anna safe and the Alpha team apprised and on the lookout for Striksky when he'd gotten word that the prince had been on his way to the States a couple of weeks ago.

Then there was the adoption and that business with Marcus Dumond's attorney when he'd ferreted out the truth of Striksky's role in Sara's death. And finally, keeping the prince's suicide hush-hush and arranging for his body to be shipped quietly back to Asterland's embassy last week had been as tricky as any litigation he'd ever handled. He was damn glad that was behind him and that explaining Ivan's demise was the government of Asterland's problem now.

So, no it wasn't the time that bothered him. It was the emotional investment he hadn't bargained for. It was the emotional investment that came with the highest price tag.

To cut his losses, he'd kept his distance from Anna. Hell, as much as possible, he'd kept his distance from Royal, flying to Dallas, or Houston and even a couple of trips to Georgia to tidy up some legal ends at the Hunt aircraft plant. Much to his friends' dismay, he'd also kept his own counsel where Anna was concerned.

Seeing her like this though—hovering on the ragged edge of a nightmare, clinging valiantly to a pride that she didn't realize her vulnerability undercut—the cost of his bid to stay away from her climbed a little higher.

He'd been skirting her like a wolf circling a fire, avoiding all but the most necessary encounters. And even though Ivan was no longer a threat, when her alarm had sounded a few minutes ago, his heart had pumped into overdrive. He'd rammed the gas pedal on his truck to the floor and flown across town to get to her.

He could see now that she was safe. She was safe, but she was far from all right. Her green eyes were wild with residual fear. He had little doubt that if she could manage to pry her fingers off the door, they'd be trembling like leaves in a windstorm.

He'd seen her like this before—on the night the Alpha team had stolen her out of Obersbourg, then a week ago when he'd broken the news that Striksky was dead. He hadn't been able to turn his back on her then. As much as his better judgment warned him against it, he couldn't do it now, not and live with himself—a characteristic that may yet prove to be his fatal flaw where Anna was concerned.

Steeling himself against the urge to fold her into his arms and hold her until her trembling stopped or until he initiated something they'd both be sorry about later, he very gently pried the slim fingers that had gone white off the door. Knowing he'd regret it, he opened it wide enough to accommodate his shoulders and slipped inside.

After shutting the door behind him and disarming the alarm panel, he turned back to her. "You got any of that sissy mint tea you managed to get Harriet hooked on?"

Her lips trembled only slightly as she gave him the small smile he'd been hoping for.

"I think I can scare some up." Brushing her hair back from her face, she headed for the kitchen.

He'd congratulated himself a hundred times for deploying Harriet Sherman—"Tank" to those who had worked with her before she'd retired from the military— next door to Anna in the role of watchdog in the guise of nosy neighbor, motherly confidante and baby-sitter. With Harriet nearby the past four months, he'd slept a little easier knowing Striksky had very quietly launched a worldwide search for Anna. In this last dark week since Striksky, faced with international humiliation when his underhanded scheme had failed, had committed suicide not five miles from Royal, he'd been doubly glad to have Harriet in place to help Anna through that ugly mess.

It was obvious to him now, however, that she was still struggling with the backlash. Standing in the arched doorway of her small kitchen, he set his jaw, told himself he'd stay long enough to make sure she was steady again. Then he'd get the hell out of the combat zone.

In the meantime, he had to work hard at snuffing out a hundred intimate details that made up the immediate moment. Like the fact that he was alone with her— something he'd managed to avoid until now. Like the fact that it was the middle of the night, the hour of shared beds, shared warmth and shared bodies. Like the damnable itch on the palms he clenched as tight as his jaw to keep from reaching out to touch her milk-white shoulder. A shoulder that was bare beneath the thin silk strap of her short, clingy nightgown. Skin that radiated a honey scent, which beckoned, enticed and clung to the midnight air like fragrance on a rose.

He knew what that skin felt like beneath his fingers, against his tongue. He knew how she tasted. What it felt like to lose himself deep inside her—like drowning in heated silk, like sinking into sweet, tight oblivion. And every night since she'd been in Royal—her safely tucked away in her apartment, and him wherever his nocturnal wanderings took him—he'd remembered every intimate detail of the love they had made.

He bit back a low growl of frustration at the turn of his thoughts. Yet when he saw that her hands were still trembling violently in the aftermath of her nightmare, he took two stalking strides toward her.

"Sit," he demanded and made himself grip her shoulders at arm's length. In a no-nonsense motion, he guided her to a chair and sat her down. "How often does this happen?"

She sat as still as a block of wood, her hands clutched tightly in her lap. "Just…not often."

Not often, my ass, he thought with a dark scowl. He'd bet his portfolio this was a nightly occurrence. Swearing as much at the clench of sympathy he felt in his chest as at his body's reaction to the way her deep breath stretched the pale-blue silk tight over the softness of her breasts, he turned back to the counter and slammed around filling the teakettle.

When he'd set it on to boil and settled himself, he turned back to her. Leaning his hips against the counter, he crossed his arms over his chest and tucked his hands under his armpits, where they wouldn't lead him into trouble.

"You don't lie worth a damn, Your Highness."

Immediately regretting the angry edge he'd let creep into his voice, he worked at gentling his tone. "You want to talk about it?"

Eyes downcast, she gave a small, tight shake of her head.

Fighting a crushing awareness of her vulnerability, he stared at that tumble of blond hair a long time before he was able to speak again. "You've been through a lot, Anna. Maybe you ought to consider seeing someone…a doctor or someone to help you through this."

"I don't need a doctor," she bristled, lifting her chin and gracing him with a valiant, aristocratic smile. "Besides, how would it look? A von Oberland in therapy? It wouldn't do. Appearances at all costs you know. Wouldn't want the world to get wind that the royal blood was anything but true blue."

He narrowed his eyes, studied her long and hard. A little starch looked good on her. It was a sign she was still fighting. Suddenly he didn't feel so bad about baiting her with the "Your Highness" crack, even though anger had provoked it. The fact was, like it or not, he had a lot of anger built up inside where Princess Anna was concerned. He'd held it in check for four years, but ever since he'd brought her here, he'd felt it escalating.

It seemed like forever instead of mere months that he'd been fighting feelings he didn't want to admit to and blaming her for being the cause. He'd done his duty. He'd gotten her out of Obersbourg, then watched from afar, made sure she was safe. Just like he'd made sure she was set up in this apartment in his own building, that she was absorbed into the small community of Royal as Annie Grace, a distant cousin of some city father too far removed for anyone to question in any depth. He'd seen her dressed in her hot-pink waitress uniform, with her hair pulled back into a nondescript pony tail, waiting tables at the local greasy spoon—a job he'd set up for her. A job he'd secretly hoped she would find appalling and so far beneath her she would have stomped her regal foot and thrown a royal tantrum.

In retrospect, he wasn't too proud of himself for stooping so low as to want to humiliate her. Not that his plan had worked, anyway. She hadn't done one damn thing he'd expected.

What she'd done was adjust. Without comment. Without complaint—and he'd been the one left feeling devalued.

She'd taken to the waitress role as if she'd been born with an order pad in her hand instead of a gilded rattle. She'd waited tables, laughed with the locals and looked and acted like she'd enjoyed every minute of it.

Act is the key word here, he told himself, working hard to reinforce his cynicism where she was concerned. He didn't dare forget that she was a consummate actress—had played the role of her life when she'd made him fall in love with her.

He rolled a shoulder, shook it off. That was then. This was now. And love—whatever the hell that was—didn't have anything to do with what he was feeling for her now. What he was feeling for her now, he told himself, was a grudging tolerance that had gotten tangled up in a misplaced sense of responsibility. And a leftover sexual obsession that he had no intention of indulging.

Stone-faced, he turned toward the whistle of the kettle, set it off the heat and snagged a pair of mugs from her cupboard. As he held the chunky stoneware in his hand, he worked hard to convince himself that the princess was no doubt missing the delicacy and the elegance of her seventeenth century fine bone china and the servants who all but drank her tea for her. Yet when he set the mug in front of her, she cupped it gratefully between her small hands, absorbed the welcome warmth, first through her fingertips then with her mouth, as she touched the mug to her lips.

A knot of tension that was becoming all too familiar when he was around her coiled tight in his gut.

"I'm fine now." She made a forced attempt to sound more steady, more centered. "You don't have to baby-sit me. People have bad dreams. It's not a big deal."

A muscle in his jaw worked involuntarily and he stated the facts as he saw them. "And you don't have to put on some brave front. This has been hard on you. There's no shame in admitting it."

The stunned look in her eyes as she reacted to his unexpected empathy momentarily silenced them both.

"Right," she said finally. "No shame."

Her voice so full of the shame she was trying to deny, it made his chest hurt.

She sat so still. Her slender fingers were wrapped around that mug like it was her only anchor. Her gaze was focused on something much further away than the clock on the far kitchen wall. And her voice, when she finally spoke, sounded as weary as time.

"I wanted Ivan out of my life," she all but whispered into a silence that had grown heavy and thick. "I'd prayed he would be made to pay for whatever part he played in Sara's death, for holding Sara's babies hostage." She lifted eyes glittering with unshed tears, stared at a time and place far away from Royal, Texas. "God help me, I wanted him dead."

The guilt etched on her face clogged his throat with emotion. He swallowed it back. Waited.

Haunted eyes flicked to his then quickly away. "I'm glad he's dead. For everything he'd done, everything he tried to do. I'm glad he's dead," she repeated and once again, met his eyes. Once again, she looked away as if she was ashamed. "What does that make me? What kind of monster does that make me?"

Everything she wouldn't let him see in her eyes was manifested in those self-indicting words, in the thready hopelessness of her voice. He wanted to drag her into his arms and hold her so she wouldn't splinter in a million pieces. Yet he sensed that if he touched her now, she would shatter. Like a beautiful spun glass swan. Like a priceless crystal vase.

Since he didn't think that both of them together could gather all the pieces if she fell apart, he made his voice as gentle as he knew how.

"What it makes you is human, Anna. It makes you human—nothing more. Nothing less. The prince was an opportunist. He was a murderer. And he was a coward—he proved it when he jumped off the bridge south of town. You had no part in that. You had no part in anything he did."

Despite the sense of his argument, her silence told him she felt she had played a very huge part in it. The next words out of her mouth confirmed it.

"If I had married him he'd be alive, though, wouldn't he? Sara might even be alive—"

It galled him to hell and back that she would take even an ounce of blame on her slim shoulders. He drew a deep breath, laid a hand on her arm. "Look—"

She jumped as if she'd been burned. "It's all right," she insisted abruptly. So abruptly he could only stare as she shook off his touch and rose. "I'm sorry...I'm sorry the alarm bothered you. I'm sorry I laid all this on you. But it's all right now. I'm all right now."

She was out of the kitchen and racing for her front door so quickly he was left standing flat-footed in his anaconda boots and a scowl. He glanced at his raised hand, curled his fingers slowly into a loose fist.

Fine, he decided, accepting that his touch had set her off. Obviously, she didn't want him here any more than he wanted to be here. And as sure as hell was fire, he didn't want to get all tangled up in caring about her again.

"Call Harriet if you need anything," he said gruffly and headed for the door. Shouldering past her, he swung it wide.

He wouldn't have thought anything could have kept him from barreling out of her apartment. Not her tears. Not her guilt.

He hadn't counted on her touch.

It stopped him cold. It stopped his heart.

Very slowly, he turned his head, looked down at the small hand that lay so tentatively on his arm, then into the eyes of the one woman who could turn hard muscle to yearning flesh, turn simple heat to complex need.

Through all of this, if there had been contact—as minimal and necessary as it had been—he'd been the one to initiate it. He hadn't initiated this. Just like he hadn't initiated the explosion of memories her singular act had stirred. *Slender hands trailing down the arch of his bare spine, delicate fingers tracing the point of his hip, tangling in his hair, caressing him, urging him closer, demanding him deeper.*

He closed his eyes, clenched his jaw so tight he heard a dull pop. Then her whispered, "I'm sorry, Gregory. I'm so sorry for everything," as her fingers drifted slowly away.

For a long moment he stood there. Struggling for something to say. Reaching for something to do. The better part of wisdom, however, overrode either instinct.

"Lock the door behind me," he ordered in a rusty voice and strode into the hall without a backward glance. He hit the apartment stairs at a jog and bounded down them and into the night. The urgency of his need to get away from her was suddenly more powerful than the one that had had him shooting across town to get to her.

When he reached his truck, he settled his hat lower on his head and ducked into the cab. Then he cranked the key, slammed into gear and hit the gas with a squeal of tires and a need for speed.

Heading across town, he refused to acknowledge that the rapid drum of his heart had to do with anything but anger for the job he was letting her do on his head. It had nothing to do with wanting to hold her. Nothing to do with needing her. Nothing, absolutely nothing to do with wishing she wasn't who she was—unreachable, untouchable, unattainable.

Like an automaton, Anna went through the motions of locking up behind Gregory. With her hand still clutching the knob, she turned and leaned back against the door. Dropping her head against its solid weight, she closed her eyes and tried to pull herself together.

The nightmare may have unsettled her, but Gregory's dark, brooding presence in her kitchen had all but undone her. His touch, so unexpected, had been the final blow. She'd had to get some distance from him.

It was hard, so hard to see him like this—controlled, distant, remote—when once they had been in love.

Well, he didn't love her now. The true irony was that four years ago she'd seen to it that he never would.

She'd known then, as she knew now, that the rebellious spirit she loved so much about him would have been broken if he had become engulfed in the circus that was her life. The stiff, orderly world of royal protocol that was too rigid, too stifling, too constricting would have emasculated him.

Her greatest gift—and her greatest sacrifice—had been to convince him that what they'd shared had been little more than a lark. That he would never fit in, in her world. To make him believe, for his sake, that there was no love binding them when, in truth, she'd ached with it since the day she'd turned and walked away.

So no. She'd seen to it that he didn't love her.

Yet he had come to her, some small corner of her heart argued as she pushed away from the door and walked slowly back to the kitchen. When he thought she was in danger, he had come to her.

Out of duty, her sense of reality was quick to point out.

She poured more hot water into her mug to rewarm her tea. He felt responsible. Nothing more. When he looked at her, his hard blue eyes relayed nothing but anger sullied by pity. When he spoke to her, his words expressed nothing but annoyance cloaked in an innate sense of kindness.

He didn't care. He wouldn't care. She'd seen to it that he couldn't afford to.

She brought the mug to her lips, sipped absently. Nothing had changed for them. Nothing *could* change for them. She'd understood that when she'd called him to come to her in Obersbourg. And yet she'd called him. And he had come. He had protected her.

Well, she was out of danger now. And where did that leave her?

She walked into the living room and curled up in the corner of the overstuffed sofa. Ivan was no longer a threat. She had kept her promise to Sara—the twins were happy with Blake and Josie. It was time to get on with her life. Obersbourg needed her. She was the only remaining hope. Somehow, she had to find a way to save her country.

As she'd told Josie at the adoption reception after hearing the new about Ivan's death, there was nothing keeping her here in Texas.

Nothing but Gregory.

It all came back to Gregory. When it came time to leave, she would like to go without looking back, but there was unfinished business between them. She owed him her life. For that, she owed him the truth. And it was the truth, when she finally worked up the courage to tell him, that would ensure he would be lost to her forever.

She stared across the empty room, as even in the face of that sobering knowledge, one recurrent thought wouldn't let go—something Gregory had said kept replaying through her mind.

"You got any of the sissy mint tea you managed to get Harriet hooked on?"

She cupped the mug fully between her palms, rubbed its warmth along her cheek. He knew what kind of tea she drank. It was a small, inconsequential detail of her life. Yet, the significance of that tiny bit of knowledge seemed, somehow, monumental. Seemed, somehow, to warm her. How could he have known what kind of tea she drank if he hadn't asked someone? And why would he ask about her, if he didn't care?

Sipping deeply, she made herself admit that she was grasping at straws. Even if he did have a small pocket of feelings for her, he would hate her when she finally told him about William.

William—who she had been forced to deny the opportunity to know his own father. Just as she had been forced to deny Gregory the right to know his own son.

A sobering dose of shame swamped her. After all that had happened—Sara's death, giving up the twins, Ivan's suicide, the burden of the secret she carried—the hurt that remained most raw was the pain of losing Gregory, both then and now.

Rising slowly, she walked back to her empty bed. She felt very alone, suddenly. Weighted with guilt, burdened by responsibility. And ready to deal with neither.

To think that once she'd believed in fairy tales. To think that once she had believed in happily ever after.

Life had shown her, however, that without qualification, no one lives happily ever after.

Not even a princess.

Three

———

It was well past 2:00 a.m. when Greg pocketed his pass
key and shut the door to the private entrance of the Cattleman's Club behind him. The Club, and the privileges
his membership afforded him, had always been a refuge.
In the past few months, it had been truly a godsend.
These days he couldn't ever seem to shake a restlessness
that kept him up late and casting about for some peace
of mind—and the Club had become his favorite haunt.

Seeing Anna so shaken a little while ago hadn't
helped the cause. Leaving her, with images of how they
had once been so good together sizzling through his
blood, had added to the mix. That's why he'd ended up
back here.

It wasn't that he didn't have enough work to keep him
busy. Hunt Industries, founded by his granddaddy and
expanded by his father, had grown to include land development and shopping malls. Under Greg's leadership,

it had also become a major player in the aviation industry. As head attorney for the entire operation, he never
lacked for work. As heir apparent to a billion-dollar fortune he'd helped create, he never lacked for motivation.
He had never been and would never be content to swing
from his daddy's shirttails. He'd worked hard to earn his
position, his reputation as a shrewd corporate counsel,
as successor to the throne of the Hunt dynasty. Sometimes he thought it had come to mean too much to him.
Sometimes he wished he could be more like his brother,
Blake, who didn't give a damn about the business.

A soft smile lifted one corner of his mouth as he made
his way to the bar in the dark, then flipped on a light
switch that cast the masculine room in muted shadows
and softly glowing light. Bit the bullet, that one had. Big
time. He still couldn't believe that his little brother, who
had played secret agent for real, who was the quintes-
sential rolling stone set on gathering no moss, was a
married man.

With a crooked smile he reached for a bottle of his
private stock of scotch. Not just married, but married
and already with a family.

At the thought of the twins, any ease of tension he'd
felt knotted tight again. It had only been a week since
Blake and Josie had celebrated the beginning of the process that would culminate in their adoption of Anna's
niece and nephew.

Anna. It all came back to her.

Grim-faced, he snagged a shot glass, poured two fingers and tossed it back. The burn of good scotch hadn't
yet cooled in his belly when he heard a door open, then
close overhead. The sound of footsteps falling on the
back stairs followed.

He'd already set a second glass on the polished surface of the bar when Hank Langley, the ex–special forces billionaire and owner of the sprawling, exclusive gentlemen's club limped into the room. The leg was bothering him again, Greg noticed with concern sullied a bit by amusement. Since Hank had hooked up with pretty little Callie Riley a few months ago, she'd seen to it that Hank didn't get much opportunity to antagonize his old war wound. Evidently, he'd snuck his dirt bike out into the hills south of town today, played "dodge the sand dunes" and riled it up some. Greg knew better than to offer sympathy or voice concern. Langley was a proud man, and though it was no failing on his part, Greg knew Hank considered the bum leg a weakness.

Hank took one look at Greg's solemn scowl and eased a hip onto a tall stool on the opposite side of the bar. "Thought you'd gone home."

"I had. Now I'm back," Greg said matter-of-factly, sliding the drink he'd already poured Langley across the bar. "What are you still doing here? Last I heard you'd turned family man—white picket fence and all that."

Hank flashed a quick grin, lifted his shot glass in salute. "I love that little girl to high heaven, and the word *family* has never had more meaning to me. But—I've lived upstairs for the better part of my adult life. When we moved out of the apartment for good, I left a little piece of me behind."

"Translated, you aren't quite ready to give up the old bachelor pad."

"Translated," Langley corrected with a wry grin, "I was feeling a need for one last little taste of a life I'd never dreamed I'd be so eager to give up—plus, I was lonesome. Callie and her aunt Manie flew out east for the weekend to visit a sick cousin," he added with a sheepish grin.

Returning his smile, Greg poured them each another shot.

Langley was quiet for a moment before angling Greg a measuring look. "So...what's up?"

Greg rolled a shoulder, noncommittal. "Couldn't sleep."

Langley nodded, stared at his glass. "Have anything to do with Annie?"

Greg hunched over his drink, considered admitting that these days everything had something to do with Anna. In the end though, he decided against answering at all. Not that it did any good.

"She okay?" Langley pressed, sensing intuitively that Anna was the catalyst for Greg's nocturnal wandering.

Greg thought of how she'd looked when he'd left her. "Yeah. She's fine." It was a bald-faced lie, but there was nothing he could do about it.

"And?" Hank prompted.

Greg shot for a negligent shrug. "And nothing."

Except for the tick of the walnut-and-brass mantel clock that lorded over the bar, the room sat heavily in silence. Deep shadows played off the rich wood paneling and crown molding of the ultra masculine club that Langley's grandfather had established nearly ninety years ago.

"Look...you can pussyfoot around the subject until dawn," Hank finally demanded, his tone making it clear he was tired of shadow dancing, "or you can spit out whatever it is that's sticking in your craw where the princess is concerned."

Greg let out a deep breath, worked his jaw.

"Okay." Despite Greg's reluctance, Hank wasn't willing to let it go. "Then I've got something to say on the subject. A man with your responsibilities doesn't drop everything, plan and help finance a mission to tote a royal princess across the Atlantic, set her up as a waitress—a damn *waitress* of all things,'' he interjected as if he could still hardly believe what Greg had done, ''and then make me believe there's nothing going on. You may want to think that whatever you had together is over, but everything you do says otherwise.

''And while you're thinking about what you're going to say about that, grab those two bottles, get yourself out from behind that bar and set with me over at that table. If I'm going to be up half the night, I mean to be comfortable.''

That said, he limped over to a walnut table arranged beneath a massive wild boar head and eased into a plush, overstuffed leather chair.

Grinning in spite of himself, Greg snagged his glass, the bottles and joined him. By the time he'd sat down and poured them both another shot, Hank had propped his bad leg on a chair and was tuning up again to ease the way.

''Hell of a deal—what's happened to her—and to that prince fella. I never did catch the whole story there.''

Greg kicked back, stacked his feet on the table and did some sorting. Facts, he could talk about. ''As you already know, Anna's country is in some financial difficulty, and her parents, the King and Queen of Obersbourg, offered her up as the prize to bail them out.''

''Nice folks.''

Greg's grim look echoed Langley's sarcasm. ''Real jewels. Anyway, Striksky was power hungry, saw Anna as a plum ripe for the picking and control over Obersbourg as the ultimate reward. When she balked at marrying him, the royal family made her a virtual prisoner in her own palace hoping she'd knuckle under.

"It's a damn bad deal what happened next. When Anna didn't come around, Striksky had a royal snit. Went off the deep end. Way off the deep end."

He paused, lifted his glass to his lips and set it down again. Swirled it slowly on the table top. "I made some contacts, had a stroke of luck and connected with the attorney who handled Marcus Dumond's estate—Dumond was Striksky's horse trainer," he elaborated. "Turns out Dumond was also the father of Anna's niece and nephew. Ivan found out about it, saw an opportunity to profit and coerced Dumond into signing an agreement that, in exchange for some mighty big money, he'd denounce his paternity."

He stopped, sipped his drink, shook his head. "Poor bastard. In effect, he signed his own death warrant. His and Sara's."

"I don't understand. And I don't understand how Anna fell into the mix. If Ivan wanted a princess, why didn't he just go after Sara?"

"Sara was too wild and willful. Striksky must have figured he'd never be able to control her. But Anna, Anna was always the dutiful little princess—and he had his mind set on her."

"That still doesn't explain what Dumond's paternity disclaimer had to do with anything."

"The disclaimer cleared the way for Ivan to claim to be the twins' father, which made them his heirs, which, in Ivan's mind, increased his leverage over Anna, who became their guardian once Sara was out of the way.

"Yeah," he said, when Langley's stunned look told him he'd finally put it all together. "We've got some pretty solid evidence that Striksky arranged for their deaths."

"And with Sara out of the way," Hank concluded, "he tried to use the twins to get to Anna."

Greg nodded. "And once he got Anna, he got Obersbourg, which was his ultimate goal." He grunted in disgust. "Because of that convoluted, tyrannical logic, both Sara and Dumond died, and when the way was clear to claim the twins as his, Ivan had all the license he needed to take them to his little toy country."

"Asterland, or something, isn't it?"

"Yeah. Asterland. Guess Striksky figured if he held the babies hostage, Anna would finally come around to help them and marry him."

Langley considered his whiskey, then Greg. "So that's when she called you to come and help her."

Greg nodded.

"And now the prince is dead."

Another nod.

"And Annie's feeling responsible," Langley concluded, thoughtful. "Poor kid. Losing her sister. Giving up those babies. Having to deal with the mess of Striksky's suicide. Don't imagine it's over yet, either. If the press gets wind of a European prince doing himself in in the middle of nowhere Texas, this place will be crawling with reporters trying to ferret out the reason why."

"I don't think we have to worry about that. These blue bloods don't like scandal. They've managed to keep Anna's disappearance from Obersbourg under wraps to save face." He let out a disgusted snort. "As far as I know, the coldhearted bastards didn't even care what Striksky was up to. They just wanted Anna to marry him to bail them out."

Langley eyed Greg thoughtfully. "At the risk of repeating myself, for a man who claims not to give a damn, sure seems to be a lot of fire in your words where she's concerned.''

Greg cut him a quick, hard look. "Don't go looking for something where there's nothing."

"Nothing?"

Greg slowly shook his head. "Nothing," he repeated firmly, then downed the last of his drink.

"Which still doesn't explain why you went after her when she called you."

Greg considered his friend, considered an excuse, then opted for leaving as the easy way out. He stood. "Sorry I got you up."

"Cute little fella." Langley stared casually at the toe of his boot and ignored Greg's sudden, pressing need to leave. "That boy of hers. Kinda quiet for a kid, though. Sorta sad, don't you think?"

Greg fished his keys out of his jeans pocket as a picture of Anna's little boy—solemn blue eyes, silent as a whisper—appeared and stayed in his mind. "Hadn't thought about it," he lied. "Guess good manners are just bred into him."

"Royal blood doesn't breed the boy out of the boy," Langley insisted, his eyes on Greg now. "He's too quiet, you ask me. Why do you suppose that is?"

"Don't know. Don't want to know. It's none of my business."

It was one more lie that felt prickly on his tongue, but he didn't want to admit that he was concerned, too. Even more, he didn't want to admit that he'd sensed a sadness in both Anna and the boy that transcended their current dilemma and wore on his defenses like the constant West Texas wind eroded the soil.

"See ya around," he said, skirting the issue. "And if I was to worry about someone, I'd worry about old fools who think they're young fools and go riling old bones on young men's toys,'' he added with a grin as Langley rose and limped toward the door to see him out.

"Go to hell, Hunt," Hank said good-naturedly. "I'm not that old and I can damn well take care of myself."

"If you can't, I know one sweet little lady who can."

"Well, that there is a bona fide fact." Grinning, Hank slapped Greg on the back. "Now get the hell out of here so I can get some sleep. And think about what you're doing where the princess is concerned. Think about what you might be letting go of—again."

That said, he closed the door and left Greg standing outside in the dark.

Hank's words trailed after him, chased him all the way across town. As he made the silent trip across Royal to Pine Valley, the exclusive private-gated residential community where he'd built his Gregorian-style mansion a couple years ago, Greg couldn't stop thinking about what Langley had said. Or about the lies he'd told him. The lies he'd been telling himself since he'd gotten Anna's phone call four months ago.

Anna's phone call.

That's all it had taken. One damn phone call and his life had suddenly become one huge lie. He'd spent the last four years trying to get her out of his head. If he was going to be one hundred percent truthful, he'd admit that it hadn't taken seeing her again to accept that he hadn't been successful. Royalty was news, and news sold everything from magazines to newspapers. Hardly a week went by that Anna's face or that of her notorious sister, Sara, wasn't splashed across the front page of a tabloid, plastered across the cover of a glitzy magazine.

So, no, he hadn't forgotten her, though Lord knew, he'd wanted to. And Lord knew, he'd tried.

He'd been twenty-seven when he'd met her. Even then, he'd been his own man. Born to old Texas money and obscene wealth, he'd been raised in a regimented but loving environment, and while not altogether bucking family tradition, he'd always done things his own way. That's why, after he'd finished law school, he'd done something as blue collar as enlist in the marines. Not just to test his own mettle, but to impress upon his father that he would make his own choices, call his own shots. It was while he was on his last tour of duty and on leave in Obersbourg that he'd met Anna.

He clenched his fingers tighter on the wheel and reluctantly gave in to the memories of the few short nights they had shared as lovers. In retrospect, he thought, stroking his thumb across the supple leather of the wheel, it had been one of the happiest times of his life.

Until she'd pointed out to him that he wasn't from her world…couldn't be a part of it. His memory flashed on the moment they'd parted, him angry, her with tears shimmering in her eyes—and over seven hundred years of aristocracy, wealth and privilege an impenetrable wall between them.

Well, old buddy, he reminded himself as he turned in his drive and hit the remote to open the iron gates that protected his property and his privacy. Just like this security gate, the wall was still there. Would always be there.

Just because she'd breezed back into his life, it didn't mean she wouldn't be breezing right on out again. As far as he could see, with Striksky dead, the only thing keeping her in Texas now was her attachment to her sister's twin babies. And now that she'd given them up to Blake and Josie, she was free of that obligation.

Only he didn't get the sense that she felt it was an obligation. He'd gotten the sense that giving them up had been very painful for her, even though by all appearances she seemed delighted with the arrangement.

So what part was she playing this time, he asked himself as he parked the truck beside his Mercedes-Benz in the garage. Was she hiding her grief over the loss of the twins or was she relieved to be rid of them?

As much as he'd like to believe the latter, when he finally hit the sheets about 3:30 a.m., he accepted that Josie and Blake had probably been right. They'd told him Anna's attachment to the twins was strong and that her struggle with her decision to give them up had been heartbreaking to witness even as they had prayed she would agree to the adoption.

It still didn't change a thing. She was from one world. He was from another. And Royal, Texas, with its common folk and simple lifestyle was a far cry from Obersbourg and life inside the gilded frame of aristocracy.

No matter how well she seemed to have adapted, there was no room in Royal for a princess and her sad little miniature prince. Just like there was no room in Obersbourg for a Lone Star prince.

Still, he drifted off to sleep thinking of a pair of summer-green eyes and the promise he'd once seen in them. He drifted off, wondering if he was wrong, if there actually could be a possibility, however slim, of something as elusive as happily ever after.

The festive sound of Christmas music had been playing nonstop at the Royal Diner since the beginning of the week. Above the music, the tinkle of the little gold bell hanging over the entrance door brought Anna's head around. Her mind automatically geared up to count heads then gather menus to take to the new table of breakfast customers.

On this bright December morning, however, there was only one head to count. Only one pair of eyes, as blue as the West Texas sky, unreadable and brooding, met hers from beneath the brim of a coal-black Stetson.

They were eyes she recognized too well. They were eyes that had once mellowed with warmth, once heated with hunger. And subjected to their probing depths, all thoughts of issuing a chipper good morning and taking another order slipped from her mind like snow sliding down Mt. Obersbourg in a sun melt.

"Mornin' Annie," Gregory said in that slow, deep, velvet-and-sandpaper voice that had mesmerized her from the beginning.

"Good morning," she managed, lost in the reality of his presence as he stood by the entrance, backlit by a rope of glittering gold garland and a row of smiling Santas that decorated the windows and door.

It shouldn't have felt so good to see him again. It shouldn't have seemed so significant. But it was good to see him. And it was significant. Over a week had passed since he'd answered her alarm and shown up a her door. Over a week had passed since she'd made her decision to tell him about William and then return to Obersbourg and get on with her life.

Yet here she was. Still in Royal. Still at the diner, where she no longer needed to hide. Still playing a part because she wasn't ready to face the reality that was her life. She was stalling for time. Praying for a miracle. Seeing Gregory like this, so unexpectedly, so wonderfully strong and vital and…yet so distant, caused a knot of tension to tighten every cell in her body. Seeing him made her realize there was no miracle on her horizon in the immediate future.

She had to tell him. She had to tell him soon. First, though, she had to work up the courage. His appearance this morning was a glaring reminder that she was running out of time.

It wasn't that he hadn't been to the diner since she'd started working here. He'd come in once or twice with his brother, Blake, or with a group of men to argue politics over coffee, talk business over breakfast. But she'd always gotten the sense that he'd been cornered into coming. And he'd always made it a point to avoid her by sitting in Sheila's section instead of hers.

Something about the way he stood there, though, in no hurry to break eye contact, made her think he wasn't particularly interested in clarifying any points today. His bold blue eyes met and held hers for such a long moment that she physically felt the pull. Her heart reacted. Then her hand, as in a knee-jerk feminine gesture, she raised it to her hair and self-consciously tucked a stray strand back into the ponytail she had hastily assembled before coming to work at 6:00 a.m.

The most remarkable thing happened then. Those hard eyes that seemed to see clear through to her soul softened. The rigid line of his mouth relaxed into what—in a benevolent stretch of imagination—could almost be taken for a smile.

It *was* a smile, she decided, and felt an absurd crimson blush creep hotly across her cheeks as he touched a finger to his hat brim, dipped his head in a subtle gesture that could have meant he was glad to see her, then walked to a booth—in Sheila's section.

It all happened so fast she was left standing there won-

dering if she'd imagined it. As he walked away, she stole
another glance at his dark profile, satisfied, as she always
was when she saw him, that he had changed very little
in the years since she'd left him alone in the plaza where
they had met. He was leaner, perhaps. The chiseled an-
gles of his handsome face were more richly defined. The
crease between his brows was deeper, the cleft in his
chin that still fascinated her, more pronounced. His face
was bold and full of character, the dark wings of his
brows hooded the stunning blue of eyes darkened by
experience and, she thought sadly, by a measure of cynicism. She sincerely hoped she hadn't been the cause.

His hair was longer now than when they'd met and
thick like sable. In their breathless flight from Obersbourg and on the few occasions she'd seen him since,
she had noticed that it had a tendency to wave, just a
little, enhancing the style, lending a sensual vulnerability
that undercut the firm set of his mouth. It was a mouth—
with that devastatingly captivating pleat in the center of
its lower lip—she remembered well, once quick with a
smile, eager to relax with laughter or seduce with a kiss
she could neither resist nor deny.

A delicious and entirely inappropriate little shiver of
desire eddied down her spine as she remembered the feel
of his lips on hers, the taste of him, the weight of him.
With a clarity that hurried her heart, she saw them together as they had been four years ago. She saw the
sunlight caress his beautiful face beside hers on the pillow the first morning she had awakened in his bed.
They'd made love all night. Glorious, lusty, delicious
love. He'd smiled at her, that slow, satisfied, I'm-
hungry-for-you-again sort of smile and reached for her.
His jaw had been morning stubbled, his hands had been
callused and so, so clever as he'd pulled her beneath

him, then tracked slow, biting kisses across her throat, to the slope of her breast, then down in languid, torturous inches to the heat of her, the heart of her...

With an abrupt shake of her head, she jarred herself back to the moment. To the ever-present and hollow ache his absence in her life had left behind. To the reality that she would never know him in that way again.

Thankfully, for the next hour, she was too busy to wonder about or even watch Gregory as a group of men—Langley, Churchill, Cunningham and Blake among them—joined him at his table. The door opened again and then again as if someone had released the floodgates and everyone in Royal had decided to have breakfast at the diner. Soon, all the other tables in the café were full as well, while "Jingle Bell Rock" played joyfully in the background.

An hour and a half later, her orders were all filled, the place was quieting down to the soft din of coffee cups on heavy restaurant-grade china and the scattered laughter of everyday Americana in Royal, Texas.

It was a peace she had grown to enjoy—even relish. The rush was over. She'd done a good job. Bellies were full, fresh coffee was brewing and, as an added bonus, Gregory was nearby—then all hell brook loose.

"Oh, man," she heard an unfamiliar male voice all but shout with unbridled joy. "I told you it was her. Jackson—are you with me? Damn it, man! I don't see any flashbulbs snapping. Get the picture. Get the damn picture!"

Four

Anna turned toward the commotion at the diner's front door. A weaselly little man wearing plaid pants and wielding a portable microphone was on a collision course in her direction. He looked as out of place among the sea of Stetsons and western shirts as tennis shoes with a tuxedo.

An old familiar fear skittered down her spine as, slippery as a shark, he hurriedly skirted several tables to get to her. Behind him, a bearded photographer snapped pictures as if he was covering a coronation.

"Beautiful!" the weasel purred, his voice dripping with smarmy greed. "Man, this is just beautiful! Princess—Princess Anna von Oberland." He flashed a business card under her nose and slung an arm around her shoulders as if she had just become his private property. "Herkner. Willis Herkner, of the *American Investigator*, at your service, Your Highness.

"You'd better be getting this Jackson," he barked, cutting a sharp glance back at the photographer and dropping all pretense of charm. "A waitress. They've got her decked out like a damn waitress!" He whooped with absolute glee before turning an oily smile back to her. "Now, Princess. Tell me. What's a nice little royal like you doing in a dump like this, huh?"

Anna was so startled by his piranha attack and his use of her title, she was at a momentary loss for words—as was everyone else occupying the Royal Diner. She darted a quick glance around the café. Everyone was staring. And she could see in their eyes that they were as shocked as they were curious. As confused as they were uneasy.

These people were her friends. At least, she had deluded herself into believing they were her friends. Suddenly she saw herself through their eyes. And through their eyes, she felt their sense of her betrayal.

"You...you're mistaken. My name is Annie. Annie Grace," she murmured miserably, the lie sounding as convincing as a snail claiming speed.

"Oh, come on. Princess. Baby. Don't play games with me. Your little jig is up. Now talk to me. Let's hammer out a deal before the rest of the pack closes in. I want an exclusive and I'm willing to pay for it."

The abrupt tinkle of the bell over the diner's front door attracted all eyes.

"Sonofabitch," Herkner snarled when a full camera crew carrying equipment with the logo of a major cable TV network burst inside. Right behind them more reporters clamored to get through the door, butting against each other like a giant logjam bottlenecked at a narrow dam.

"Come on, Princess!" Herkner grabbed Anna by her

arm, broke into a trot and dragged her with him toward the diner's back door. "This story is mine. I'll be damned if I'll let those other bloodhounds beat me out of it. Talk to me. What are you doing hiding out here? And what do you know about the death of Prince Ivan Striksky? That's right," he said, malicious accusation widening his shark's smile when she planted her feet and jerked out of his grasp. "We know about that. We know that he followed you here and now he's dead. Here's your chance to tell your story. Now give."

Gripping her arm painfully, he started dragging her with him toward the back of the diner again. Even as he pummeled her with questions, the flood of reporters and photographers continued to glut the café, began to catch up with them, engulfing her in an endless, battering barrage of shouts and flashbulbs.

Manny poked his head out over the cook's counter as an artificial Christmas tree toppled to its side in the ruckus. "What the hell's going on?"

Anna grabbed hold of a table for an anchor as they passed by.

"Manny!" She sought his eyes and his help even as he vaulted over the counter and tried to cut his way through the crush toward her.

But it was hopeless. Herkner jerked her free and yanked her toward the rear exit. There were too many of them—and only one of Manny.

"Hold them off, Manny!"

Anna's gaze shot up as the sound of Gregory's voice rose above the chaos of yelling reporters and the bump and scrape of tables and chairs being shoved out of their way. Her heart cried with hope as she spotted his black Stetson above the crowd, then dove into despair when he got stalled in the middle of the jam of bodies.

He didn't stay in the crush for long. With an agile stride, he stepped up on a chair, from the chair he leaped onto a table. And then he was rushing toward her, literally leaping from tabletop to tabletop. Candles wreathed with holly berries, napkin holders, salt and pepper shakers and anything else in the way flew as the good folk of Royal ducked under booths and dove out of the way.

If it hadn't been so frightening, it would have been laughable. It was like a scene from one of those cops-and-criminal movies she sometimes let William watch when she didn't have the heart to turn off the TV. The whole diner was in a collective state of mayhem. A popular country artist launched into "Rudolph the Red Nose Reindeer" as Herkner dragged her farther away from Gregory.

His grip on her arm was brutal. The army of reporters and camera crews lurching forward in hot pursuit was relentless. And Gregory, gaining on the whole ugly swarm, maneuvered around hanging tinsel and wobbly tables to get to her side.

Forrest Cunningham and Sterling Churchill, she realized, had joined the mix, too. So had Blake. She caught glimpses of them close behind Gregory, striding briskly over tables and booths in their cowboy boots, expertly dodging the grabbing hands of the reporters, throwing in a shoulder block here, a body slam there, guarding Gregory's back as, stone-faced, he made his way to her side.

Langley had also come to his friend's aid. He'd stationed himself like a cement wall by the front door. The black look on his face and the fever of the fight glinting from the eyes shielded by the brim of his hat invited the late arrivals to just try to get past him and get inside.

"Let her go, you sleazebag!" Gregory snarled as he

hooked an arm around Herkner's neck. When the reporter jerked viciously on Anna's arm, Greg brought a knee up hard in his left kidney.

Herkner groaned like a dog with a bellyache and let go. "That...that's...assault. I'll...s-sue," he croaked miserably then folded like a tin roof in a hurricane wind.

"So I'll see you in court," Greg shouted as Herkner doubled over into a ball on the floor. Stepping over him, Gregory tucked Anna against his side. "While we're at it, we'll have a little chat with the judge about invasion of privacy. And how about throwing a little attempted kidnapping into the mix just for fun?"

With Gregory's arm around her, strong, yet gentle, he made a shield of his body and sheltered her from the rapidly gaining pack.

Caught up in the frenzy of the mob mentality, a freckle-faced reporter who saw headlines instead of danger broke through the throng and got within three feet of Anna.

"You just entered the danger zone, partner!" Manny warned, blocking his way.

"Chill out, man." He hefted his camera and shot, fast and furious. "Don't you know it's always open season on princesses?"

"I know it's open season on skunk," Manny said, then politely lopped him over the head with an iron skillet and watched with a smile as he crumbled to the floor without a whimper.

"Go! Go, man," Manny shouted to Greg, and grinning like a fallen angel, tucked into a karate stance, daring the next reporter to challenge him.

"You want a piece of Manny?" he crooned over the noise. "You just come on, you miserable little cockroaches. Let's see what you got."

"Manny! Buzzard bait at ten o'clock!"

He spun around as Sheila yelled a warning then launched herself off a chair and onto Manny's pursuer's back.

"Ride him, little Sheba!" Manny let out a whoop of laughter and dove across the sea of bodies to help her.

Anna saw it all as if it was a bad dream, as Gregory steered her closer to the back door and safety. Too late she heard a table topple beside her. She tried to dodge it, stumbled over a fallen chair and felt herself falling.

She was falling and running and the hands just kept grabbing—just like in her nightmare. But no sooner was she hit by the sensation of being sucked into a quicksand of seeking hands was she being lifted off her feet. With a cry of relief, she wrapped her arms around Gregory's neck, buried her face against the solid strength of his chest and clung to the haven she had thought she'd never find.

The next sound Anna heard was the solid thump of the diner's back door slamming shut behind them. The next sensation she felt was the brilliance of the Texas sun on her cheek and the heat of Gregory's body against her breast. And the next time she opened her eyes, she was still wrapped in Gregory's arms, his heart beating fast and heavy against hers.

They flew down the alley, Gregory running like an Olympic sprinter. He ducked around a corner, checked the street for reporters. When he spotted several milling around the diner's door, he swore under his breath. Gauging the distance, he sucked in a deep breath and made a break for his truck.

When he reached it, he jerked opened the driver's side door and tumbled Anna inside. He'd just hitched a hip onto the seat and reached for the ignition when a CNN photographer with a video camera blocked the door.

"Back off!" Greg snarled.

"In your dreams, cowboy." The photographer stuck the lens in the open door to get a better shot.

Mistake. Big mistake.

With a roar of pure, primal rage, Greg jerked the camera out of his hands.

"Hey—that's private property. You can't—"

He stopped midsentence when the camera flew over his head and into the street in front of the truck.

Without missing a beat, Greg cranked the key and rammed the truck in gear. Peeling away from the curb, he deliberately ran over the expensive camera.

"My camera! You killed my camera!" the reporter wailed as Greg gunned the motor, shifted directly from first to fourth gear and burned rubber for three blocks.

Stunned into silence, Anna hung on to the seat with one hand and brushed the hair that had tumbled from her ponytail out of her face with the other. With a shaky breath, she glanced behind them. The throng of reporters clambered out of the café and into their vehicles.

"They're following us!"

"They can try," Greg muttered, cutting a quick glance to the rearview mirror. His expression, odd as it seemed under the circumstances, could have passed for a smile. "Buckle up. This is *not* going to turn into a parade."

He downshifted, hit the brake and the gas at the same time and jetted them in a screeching, careening, two-wheel, ninety-degree turn around the corner. Shifting straight into fourth gear again, he punched the accelerator and sent them flying.

If her jaws hadn't been locked so tight she'd have

screamed. Loud and long. Buildings bled by in blurry images as they raced across town. Every intersection was an exercise in nerve as he ran stoplights, dodged cars, then did another one of those flying ninety's. This time they ended up sandwiched in a narrow alley, where he tucked the pickup neatly between an idling garbage truck and a brick wall.

Greg kept the motor revved and his eyes glued on the rearview mirror. A tense five minutes passed before he let out a long breath and turned his gaze to Anna.

The adrenaline from the exhilaration of the cat-and-mouse chase bottomed out at the look of her. Damn. She looked bruised, battered and about two breaths away from shattering like glass.

The freckle-faced reporter's words came back like a tabloid headline: *"It's always open season on princesses."*

For the first time since this all began, Greg let himself feel a full dose of pity for the fishbowl life Anna had to endure. At the same time, his mind geared down long enough to remember the feel of her in his arms when he'd carried her out of the diner.

It had been four years since he'd held her. Four years since he'd felt the sweet yielding warmth of her body nestled against his. It had been four damn years too long.

He tightened his grip on the wheel. "I think we lost them," he said when what he wanted to do was pull her into his arms and hold her again.

She nodded, looking straight ahead.

A sudden concern outdistanced his desire. "Anna, are you okay?"

Another nod, but slow enough in coming that he felt a sharp, hard pain somewhere in the vicinity of his heart. "Did that bastard hurt you?"

She pinched her eyes shut. Touched a hand unconsciously to her arm and shook her head.

Instantly alert, he flicked open the buckle on his seat belt, twisted in the seat and pushed up her sleeve. He swore under his breath. Four angry red welts in the exact shape of a man's fingers mottled her milk-white skin. Tomorrow they'd be black and blue.

Tomorrow Herkner would be eating through a straw.

Through the rage, he saw her tear. And it was then that he lost his mind completely.

"Ah, hell." He slid over beside her. "Come here," he said gruffly, flicked open her seat belt and pulled her into his arms.

She came like a kitten. All delicate curves and snugly warmth. And he was lost. Again. Lost, still, he realized, as she curled up on his lap, wrapped her arms around his neck and held on like he was the harbor she'd been seeking in an endless sea of uncertainty.

"It's all right," he murmured. "It's all right."

He felt her tense, sensed her struggle to contain the tears, but the dam broke against her will and she started to cry openly then.

"Oh, damn. Don't. Anna, don't. Don't cry," he whispered, pressing his lips against her hair, touching them to the delicate shell of her ear, skimming them across her brow. "Please don't cry."

It was the most natural thing in the world for him to tip her face to his. He wiped her tears with his thumbs, cradled her face in his hands. And still she cried. Silent, heartbreaking tears that cost her the pride she so valued and that he knew only one way to silence.

He brushed his lips across hers, whispered her name, tasted the salt of her tears, the essence of what made her Anna, and threw caution and common sense to the wind.

He silenced her soulful sobs with a kiss. Long, strong and innately tender. He cruised his mouth over hers, soothing, gentling, promising with his touch that he'd slay dragons, scale castle walls, anything to stop this endless flow of tears and events that kept happening to her.

She cried harder at first, as if she wanted what he offered but didn't trust herself to take it. Then under his gentle onslaught, she began to settle. She began to trust—in the comfort that he offered, in the message his tenderness relayed. And she began to take what he so wanted to give.

She opened her eyes, and in their misty-green depths he saw the awakening of hunger. He saw the emergence of need. And he set about satisfying both.

He slanted his mouth over hers, protectively, possessively, taking charge, taking care. For a moment it was enough. For a moment he made it be enough—and then everything changed.

The brush of her hand on his cheek, once tentative and hesitant, became caressing and hot. The fit of her mouth beneath his, once trembling and needy, became wanton and lush. She didn't just open for him. She invited him home.

Where he'd wanted to be for four long years.

Where, at this moment, he had no doubt in the world, he belonged.

And then he was just taking. He took what she offered. He feasted on what she gave.

It was sweet. It was fine. As sweet as fresh water to a man parched on salt and sand. As fine as the raw silk of her hair that he'd tangled in the hungry fist of his hand.

He settled her more firmly on his lap, pressed the delicate fullness of her hip to his groin, let her feel the thickening length of his arousal, cruised a hand toward her breast...

The jolting bleat of a horn ripped his mouth from hers. Swearing darkly, Greg looked frantically over his shoulder for the source while he tucked Anna's face protectively against his chest.

"Take it somewhere else, buddy," a balding man with a dirty T-shirt and a fat, stubby cigar bellowed from behind the wheel of the garbage truck. "I got a schedule to keep."

When Greg could form a thought that didn't involve kissing or killing, he realized he was blocking the truck in. With unsteady hands, he set Anna off his lap and told her to buckle up again. Once he'd done the same, he shifted into low and crept toward the opening of the alley.

After checking left and right and seeing no cars that looked threatening, he eased out of the alley and onto the street.

Then he silently damned himself for his loss of control.

"I'm sorry," he said quietly. "That shouldn't have happened."

When she smoothed the hair from her face, he noticed her hand was no steadier than his. Just like he noticed the bruised look about her swollen lips and the fact that she chose to deal with his apology by ignoring it. "Where will we go?"

He slogged out a deep breath, his attention bouncing back and forth between the road ahead, the street at their backs and what had happened in that alley. "I'm not sure yet."

Another block passed by before he punched in a speed-dial number on a cell phone built into his console.

"Hunt residence," a very proper, very professional gentleman answered.

"Lawrence," Greg replied crisply, still working on pulling himself back together. "I'm en route. What's the climate out there?"

"Climate, sir?"

"Check the security cameras at the drive. Do you see any cars?"

"Just a moment, sir."

Greg filtered through the unspoken questions he saw in Anna's eyes. He ignored all but the one he thought he could deal with. "Lawrence takes care of my Pine Valley residence for me."

"Sir," Lawrence's voice came back on the line.

"What's the story?"

"An unusual number of vehicles seem to be parked outside the estate gates. More are pulling up as we speak. They appear to be television crews."

Greg swore under his breath. Herkner and his minions must have found out about Greg and the Cattleman's Club members' involvement with Anna's abduction from Obersbourg—and that he'd been providing protection for her from Ivan and lately from the press.

"Sir? Is there something I should do? Do you wish that I call the police?"

"No. Let 'em sit there and stew."

"Yes, sir. Will you be home for dinner, sir?"

He let out a weary chuckle. "Not anytime soon, Lawrence. Not anytime soon."

"Sir?"

"I'll fill you in later. In the meantime, guard the fort, Lawrence. Don't let them in."

"As you say, sir."

He broke the connection, checked his rearview again.

"Now what?" she asked, her thick lashes still heavy with the tears she had shed.

Drawing a deep breath, he slowly let it out and came to a reluctant decision. Though it was the last thing he wanted to do, he headed south, out of town. "Now we hope they don't find out about my ranch until after I've got you safely settled in."

"Ranch? You have a ranch?"

Though he wasn't pleased with his solution, he tried for a smile. "This is Texas, Anna. Of course I have a ranch."

"How...how far is it?"

"Far enough that once we give those jackals the slip, they'll play hell getting past my security."

"William," she said suddenly, her voice filled with an alarm that had been silently building. "I can't leave William."

Without a word, he punched in another speed-dial number.

Harriet answered on the third ring.

"Hey, Tank. How's it going?"

Harriet Sherman's chuckle rang out over the console speaker. "That was my line. I've had my police scanner on. Sounds like you're cutting your own grand prix route through Royal. What's going on?"

"I'll fill you in later. Right now, I need you to get yourself and Anna's little guy out of the apartment and out to the ranch. No fuss. No delays, okay?"

"Consider it done. We'll see you there in an hour then."

He'd known he could count on Harriet. She understood the need for discretion and speed—and was blessed with the good sense not to ask any questions.

"We'll be waiting."

He disconnected, cut a look Anna's way. "Okay?"

She nodded. Let out a pent-up breath. "Okay."

Only nothing was okay. And as he sped for the city limits and the wide-open spaces that led to his ranch, Casa Royale, Greg wondered if anything in his life or hers would ever be okay again.

Five

Sunlight glinted off the untidy tumble of Anna's blond hair as she raced toward Harriet's car, scooped the boy into her arms and held him close. Greg watched from the shadows of the foaling barn, a sober scowl on his face.

His sense of exclusion was acute and, in the absolute, unwarranted. Not only did he not fit into that picture, he was the one who had pulled into the drive, showed Anna into the ranchhouse, then beat a hasty retreat to the barn to get some distance from her. Like a coward. Like a man suffering from a straight, clean shot of raw emotion that burned like whiskey in his gut.

Yeah, he'd lost control in that alley, but it was the moment, he told himself in a bid to rally some pride as he headed toward Harriet's car. It was just that seeing Anna attacked by that swarm had sent a surge of adrenaline bolting through his blood. He couldn't let them mob her.

You could have kept your damn hands off her, though, he blasted himself as he covered the distance in long, slow strides. But he hadn't. He hadn't, and a part of him that couldn't squelch what they'd had together—what he'd *thought* they'd had together four long summers ago—still ached to finish what he'd started in that alley.

The sane, pragmatic, unemotional part of him, however, knew it would have come to no good end. He still had to deal with the residual damage, however—and not by hiding out in a dark horse barn in the clear blue light of day.

"Hey, Greg," Harriet said by way of greeting when she spotted him walking toward her car.

Harriet was sixty-five years old and had lived every one of them. Greg had trusted her with his life—this petite woman in her loose fitting jeans and western shirt, her salt-and-pepper hair and hard-earned crow's feet— just like he had trusted her with Anna and William's lives.

He knew before he asked that he'd had no need to worry about the latest great escape from Royal. "Have any trouble getting out here?"

"Not a lick."

"Were you followed?"

She grinned. "Only by a couple of your cronies. I believe it was Churchill and Cunningham. They must have put two and two together and figured you'd sent me this way with little Will, here."

He looked toward the heavily gated drive that was carefully camouflaged by a strategically designed land-scape of colorful, rugged boulders, squat mesquite trees, crape myrtle, yucca and yaupon. Only the mesquite were native to the area. The rest of the vegetation flourished only because of painstaking nurturing and constant care.

"They turned around a few miles back, when they were certain we'd made it without trouble." Harriet opened the back door, reached for a suitcase.

Greg cocked a brow.

"Sorry, hon. I know you said no delays. I travel light, but not that light. I had to pack my makeup mirror. And the boy had to have his jammers. Right, Will?"

Prince William von Oberland grinned shyly around the arms that held him. "Cowboys," he said, snuggling closer to his mother and sliding an uncertain look Greg's way.

"Cowboys?" he asked, at a loss.

"His pajamas," Harriet supplied, as Greg hefted the suitcase out of her hand and headed for the house. "They're Dallas Cowboys pajamas," she explained.

"Well, all right then." Greg offered the boy an open grin and, in a spontaneous reaction to his shy smile and very compelling charm of his blue eyes, ruffled his dark hair. "Glad to see you hitched your wagon to a winner, there, Wild Bill." Then he walked ahead of them to open the front door.

Silent throughout the exchange, Anna was gripped by the picture of Greg's strong, tanned hand tousling William's hair. Emotions too riotous to stall flooded her at his simple gesture of kindness. William knew so little of a man's gentle touch. Knew less of affection from that quarter. The hero worship that spread across his face when Gregory had called him Wild Bill was both sweet and painful to witness, yet a bludgeoning reminder that he knew nothing of a father's touch—until that very moment.

An ache that had started even before William was born intensified and weighed on her heart like lead.

"Telephone, Mr. Hunt."

A slim woman with warm brown eyes and a lovely, dark complexion that proudly proclaimed her Mexican heritage met them just inside the foyer.

Gregory had briefly introduced Anna to Juanita Hernandez when he'd shown her into the house earlier. Juanita smiled a welcome to Harriet and gave William a friendly wink as she handed Gregory a portable phone.

"Hunt," Greg said briskly into the receiver, and with a sweeping lift of his hand, he invited Anna and Harriet to make themselves comfortable in the great room while he took the call.

Juanita curled a finger for William to follow her. Her open smile and the delicious scents wafting from the kitchen were too compelling an enticement for William to deny. With a quick look at his mother, who gave a nod of consent, he bounced shyly off the sofa and walked toward Juanita. His ramrod-straight gait told Anna he was hesitant but determined.

"You like cookies?" Juanita invited softly as she tucked William along her side with a gently guiding hand. "My Tito likes cookies. I bet he will like you, too. Come. I'll have him show you where I keep the cookie jar."

"Juanita is Greg's housekeeper," Harriet explained, unnecessarily as the two left for the kitchen. "Her husband, Alexandro, trains Greg's quarter racers. Tito's their youngest boy. I think he's five now. Sweet child. He'll make a wonderful playmate for William while you're here."

While you're here. Anna replayed the words in her mind, wondering just how long that would be, calculating how long she could afford to stay. They'd embarked on a grave journey four months ago. Nothing to date, however, had felt more dangerous than the kiss she and Gregory had shared in that back alley a little over an hour ago. Dangerous and exciting. And totally forbidden if she was going to get out of this with her sanity intact.

When they had arrived earlier and Greg had shown her inside, she'd been too shaken by all that had happened and too worried about William to take in her surroundings. Now that he was here and safe, now that she had a little distance from the impossible pull she still felt toward Gregory, she settled onto the sofa and took a long, sweeping look around her.

The house was pure, perfect Texas. Huge rooms, open archways, sunlit alcoves. Warm blues and brick reds. Soothing shades of sand. All the colors and textures combined to lend a glow of welcome, enhance the sense of space.

From the exterior adobe walls to the stucco, brick and pine of the great room, Gregory's home looked like something that came from the earth, something that came from his own strength, an extension of his character. A towering fireplace crafted from pristine limestone dominated the great room, just as he dominated any room he was in. The same rough cedar that she'd noticed in the porch posts was repeated on the ceilings. Saltillo tile elegantly graced the gleaming foyer floor.

Heavy frontier-inspired furniture invited cushioned warmth and hospitality, while tanned cowhides and Navajo rugs accented everything from the walls to the longleaf pine floor. Every decorative touch rang true, ingraining the house with the essence of his Texas heritage, in the respect he felt for tradition. It was a home that was deeply and intrinsically attuned to the rich history of the land, land that Gregory told her when they'd passed the main entrance gate into Casa Royale had been in his family for more than a century.

She glanced toward the dining area that was open to the great room. A hand-hewn and intricately carved table and matching chairs spoke of both age and native craftsmanship and cried for a family to fill it with laughter and celebration.

Greg's dark scowl as he disconnected from his call put thoughts of celebration or the future on hold—replaced them with more pressing thoughts. The here and the now.

"Bad news?" Harriet reacted to Greg's dark look while Anna's insides coiled into tight knots.

"That was Blake. He did some checking on what prompted today's little scene in the diner. It seems there was a leak in the Asterland embassy. News of the prince's death got out a couple of days ago. The reporter—Herkner—the one who accosted you, Anna, works for the *American Investigator*—"

"The *Investigator?* That sleazy rag?" Harriet interrupted in disgust.

"That sleazy rag," he confirmed, meeting Anna's eyes, then looking quickly away. He headed for the bar in the corner of the room.

"Wasn't it the *Investigator* that broke the story last month about a possible spotting of Prince Striksky in Royal?"

"Yeah, it was. While the Alpha team kept an eye on Striksky, I did a little creative leaning on the right people and got any follow-up stories squelched. It didn't keep Herkner from asking questions, though. He eventually found out that Anna's parents and Striksky had been in league to arrange a royal wedding. When he dug deeper, he found out about Anna's disappearance, that it had been covered up. From there it was just a matter of ferreting out where Ivan died. When he did, Herkner headed for Royal, asked more questions and stumbled onto Anna working in the diner.''

"And the rest, as they say, is history," Harriet summed up tidily.

Greg opened the minifridge, found a long-neck bottle of beer and twisted off the lid. Anna expected him to tip it to his lips. Instead, he rounded the bar and extended the bottle to Harriet, who gratefully downed a healthy swallow.

When Anna declined his offer of something to drink, he returned to the bar for his own bottle of beer.

"If Herkner hadn't been so damn pleased with himself and bragged to a friend who is also a freelance reporter, we could have contained things. Bought him off and at least bought a little more time. But his mouth was bigger than his brain. Once he let the word out, it raced across the wires like a brushfire.''

"And they all descended on the diner like locusts today,'' Harriet concluded as Anna rose and walked silently to the window.

Outside was an artfully manicured lawn, beautifully littered with cactus, flower beds and miniature trees of everything from live oak to mulberry. All was within the confines of a walled fortress, whose sweeping view of the flat, desertlike prairie beyond the horse barn was out of her reach. She hugged her arms around herself. It was a beautiful prison. Nothing like the one she'd escaped in Obersbourg, but she was a prisoner here, just the same. A prisoner of the media's making.

Harriet exchanged a concerned look with Greg.

"They can't get to you here, Anna," he said, misreading her silence for fear. "I protect my property. I protect my privacy."

And I'll protect you were the words left unspoken and unnecessary in light of all he had already done.

It closed in on her suddenly that with Ivan dead, the only thing left to protect her from was her life. Her life as a princess. She'd grown up with cameras thrust in her face. She'd grown up as the center of attention. Until she'd arrived in Texas and played the part of Annie Grace, she had never had a life she could call her own. She'd been public property. Loved. Revered. Adored. But expected, always, to be available to her subjects, the paparazzi, the world.

It was selfish, she knew, to let Gregory go on protecting her when the only threat she still faced was from the life she had been born and bred by royal blood to lead. Sadder still, she couldn't rally the strength to do anything but take advantage. She would let him protect her from the encroachment of a life she had lived for twenty-eight years.

For just a little while longer. Just a little while longer, even though she felt the shame of her weakness like she felt the burden of the obligations that waited for her. Just a little longer—until she garnered the courage to tell him about William.

She glanced at Gregory. An enveloping sadness replaced the impossible yearning in her heart. Who will protect you, Gregory, she thought as she turned her gaze from his and back to the prairie beyond the walled gardens. Who will protect you from the pain when I finally find the strength to tell you of my betrayal?

Even as she posed the question, she knew there was only one answer. She, and only she, could be the one.

She would shield him from the pain by cushioning it with the gift of his son.

The thought of telling him made her heart race. He wouldn't understand. When she finally found the courage to tell him, he would never be able to comprehend her reasons for keeping William from him all these years. And while those reasons were compelling, there was no possible way for her to make it up to him.

She couldn't make it up, but she could correct it. One look at the way William's blue eyes—eyes so like his father's—lit up when Gregory had ruffled his hair in a gesture of genuine, honest affection, and she'd known she *had* to correct it for William's sake. Even if in doing so, she would risk losing William, too.

An even bigger risk, however, was the gamble she'd be taking with William's tender heart. She had no assurances that Gregory would embrace him as his own. Yes, it was apparent that Gregory was open to liking, possibly loving, William, but there were no guarantees that he would want to become an instant father of a child he had never known. To have his life cluttered with a timid little boy who was hungry for the father he deserved.

That gamble alone was enough reason to hold, for a little longer, a silence bred by a secret that had not yet run its course. She could not, would not return to Obersbourg until she was certain of Gregory's love for their child. Then and only then could she tell him.

Dawn slid across the vast West Texas horizon like the silver streak of a distant, slow moving train. No pastel butterfly emerging from a cocoon, it was all blazing light and dazzling color as the cobalt of night blended and bled, and graciously gave way to a blue so brilliant it burned.

Anna hugged a borrowed bathrobe around her and watched the sunrise from the patio in suspended awe, indulging in its spectacle and the morning quiet until the house woke up around her. Only when the delicious scents from Juanita's kitchen teased her senses did she rouse herself enough to return to the bedroom Gregory had given her. She quickly showered, then blessed Harriet, who had not only packed William's pajamas but some fresh underwear and a pair of Anna's jeans and a pale-blue cotton sweater.

Tito and William came tumbling out of the house and into the yard as Anna sat down at the table on the airy screened-in patio. A soft breeze ruffled her hair as she sat in a teak chair beneath a ceiling of hand-hewn Douglas fir beams. The bluestone floor beneath her bare feet held the coolness of the past night; embers from a fire Juanita had built last evening glowed orange-gold in the open fire pit at her back.

In the sweet shade of this vine-covered extension of the main house, she appreciated the ornamental grasses dotting the edge of a low stone fence that lead to a kidney-shaped pool. Juanita had pointed out the West Texas native sotol, a plant with narrow, serrated leaves that sent up tall flower stalks in the spring.

Spring. She wondered where spring would find her.

Her gaze swept the garden dotted with Mexican stone sculptures resembling plump turkeys and horse heads. A fountain bubbled peacefully near the sculptures, and suddenly she yearned to be sitting on one of the many stone benches circling it. William and Tito sat giggling in the grass nearby. She was about to join them when a horse disguised as a dog galloped straight toward William, who sat cross-legged with a glass of milk and a piece of Juanita's special cinnamon toast.

Alarmed by the size of the dog, Anna rose swiftly from her chair.

A strong hand gripped her wrist and stopped her.

"Leave them. They're fine."

She hadn't heard Gregory approach. Wasn't prepared for the impact of his touch. Or for the way her heart kicked up when she lifted her gaze to his as he sat down and indicated she should do the same.

She couldn't take her gaze from his face—could barely digest the words as he spoke in his slow, Texas way, his attention on the boys, avoiding eye contact with her.

"Cosmo won't hurt the boy."

"Cosmo?" Breaking the tether of his effect on her, her gaze swung back to the huge dog as he put on the brakes and parked his lumbering black self right between the boys.

When Tito laughed, William joined in. After only a little hesitation, he reached out to pet the shaggy Newfoundland, who promptly rolled over onto his back and begged for a belly rub.

Until she had brought him to Texas, William would have shied from his own shadow. Today he set his milk aside, fed Cosmo the last of his toast, then flung his arms around the dog's neck and snuggled against him as if he was a big teddy bear.

Tears stung her eyes as she watched. William's open gesture of trust was both heartwarming and humbling. As little as four months ago, he wouldn't have known how to react to the trusting affection the dog exuded.

A sad smile tilted one corner of her mouth. Four months ago, he wouldn't have been sitting in the grass in denims with frayed knees and a Cowboys T-shirt that Juanita had found for him in a box of cast-off clothes Tito had outgrown. He would have been doing what his grandparents expected of him.

It was now, as he displayed this uninhibited and open affection, that she accepted full measure what her parents' staunch, staid exceptions had done to him. And she was ashamed that she had not been more effective in undercutting their influence.

Little boys should laugh without fear of reprisal. Before he came to Texas, William rarely laughed. Little boys should run like the wind and wrestle in the dirt. William had never been allowed to get dirty.

Little boys should be little boys—not miniature men, conditioned to always display impeccable manners, to being seen and not heard, to always look like they had dressed to pay homage to a king.

And she had to take him back to all that.

Aware, suddenly, of Gregory's dark eyes on her, she made herself relax. Muscle by muscle, she let the tension flow from her body—until she made eye contact with Gregory again.

Like the dawn, Gregory Hunt was a stunning addition to the morning. Like her, he'd recently showered. Like her, he'd dressed in denims. There the similarities ended. And as they took stock of each other over the steaming plates of western omelettes and fresh melons that Juanita set before them, she'd never been more aware of those differences.

Drifting above the delicious aroma of Juanita's breakfast, a hint of scent—the deep, masculine scent of his aftershave—arrested her attention, took her back to yesterday and the kiss they had shared.

Until that moment, she had managed to keep at bay

the sweet, heated desire he had never failed to bring to flash point when they had been lovers. Until yesterday when he'd held her again, until he'd gentled her with his words, then aroused her with his touch, she had been able to keep her need for him under control. And now because she had given in, she couldn't look at him without wanting to make love to him.

She should have resisted. When he'd touched his strong, lean fingers to her face, when he'd pressed tender kisses to her brow, she should have resisted. She'd known where it would lead. She'd known and she hadn't stopped him. Couldn't have stopped him if her life had hung in the balance. For his touch, for his kiss, she would risk anything. And now it seemed she had. She'd risked her heart again, and judging by the closed look on his face, the gamble hadn't paid off.

She eased away from her dismal thoughts as Harriet joined them.

"What a fine morning." With a grin and a nod toward the boys and the dog, she sat down and poured herself a cup of coffee. "And to think, tomorrow I'll be slogging through six inches of slush and snow trying to convince myself it's pretty."

"Tomorrow?" Anna lost the battle to keep the alarm from her voice. "You're leaving?"

When Harriet turned kind eyes to her and nodded, she felt her fingers grow cold under the Texas sun.

"It's Christmas next week, honey," Harriet said gently. "My family is in New York. They expect me there."

Christmas. Family. Of course. Of course, she'd known Christmas was only a week away. She'd known Harriet would be leaving for a family visit. With all that had happened, it had slipped her mind. For someone like

Harriet, the holidays would be a time of family celebration, of homecoming and warm embraces.

She made herself smile. She hadn't realized until this moment how she had grown to depend on Harriet's genuine warmth and affection. "I'll miss you. William will miss you."

Harriet's smile hovered somewhere between affection and sorrow. "That goes both ways." She hesitated, glanced at a hard-faced Greg then back to Anna. "Will I see you here when I return to Royal after New Year's?"

Anna couldn't find it in her to meet Harriet's kind eyes. "I...I don't know. I—"

"It's all right." Harriet covered Anna's cold hands with hers. "If not here, we'll make sure we get together again soon, okay?"

It was a time-honored ploy to avoid the pain of dealing with a goodbye that neither wanted to accept. So Anna played the game, for Harriet's sake and for hers.

"Absolutely. We'll keep in touch."

Yet when Harriet left the table to join the boys and spend some time with William before she left for Royal to pack for tomorrow's flight, Anna struggled with a sad certainty that she might never see Harriet again.

Greg watched the exchange with a mood that grew blacker by the minute. This was not how things were supposed to work out. He was not supposed to feel these things for Anna—things that started with empathy, built to concern, drifted hard and heavy toward a desire he'd only pretended no longer existed.

Hell. She wasn't supposed to end up here. Not here, the one place where he'd always been able to escape to be free of her. Her sanctuary was not supposed to overlap with his.

Casa Royale had always been that. His sanctuary. His pocket of paradise carved out of the heat of West Texas. He'd never brought a woman here. Had never intended for Anna to end up here but he'd run out of options yesterday. As he watched her steel herself to deal with the pain of letting go of yet one more person who was special to her, he felt close to the end of his control as well.

Four years ago he had never planned on falling in love with her. Once he had, he'd never planned on letting her go. She was the one who had done the walking away. She was the one who had said goodbye.

Now she was back in his life. She was back, and unfortunately, every time he turned around she seemed to be more deeply rooted into his existence—like he was rooted to life in the West Texas soil. He had to remember that the soil in Texas was shallow. Transplanted vegetation did not flourish here. Like life, it had to be nurtured in order to sustain it, and it had to be resilient enough to grow.

Despite her fragile appearance, Anna was resilient. She'd proven that. But, like his carefully tended gardens, she was not native. There was little chance that she would thrive here. And he, he had no business even thinking along those lines.

Yet fool that he was, with increased involvement, came a damnably increasing need. He wanted to be the one to slay her dragons, to free her from the sadness in her heart and heal the world of hurt she tried to hide behind those fathomless green eyes.

For some unaccountable reason he didn't want to explore, he was also drawn to that quiet, tentative little boy of hers. William's reserve called out to him in a way he couldn't explain. Recurrent and unreasonable notions kept cropping up, telling him that he ought to be the one to open the locked door so the child behind those serious blue eyes could come out and play.

He was getting in too deep. Way too deep. He was letting himself get involved with thoughts of both Anna and the child that weren't his to consider.

Abruptly, he rose from the table, steeled himself against the look of her, green eyes questioning, the long, unbound silk of her hair trailing halfway down her back.

"If you'll excuse me. I have work that needs my attention."

He left her then. Walked straight to his office. Shut the door. And there, by God, he told himself he would stay until he came to his senses, or at least until he got a handle on them.

Six

"The filly's all heart and speed, Mr. Hunt. She's gonna be a good one." Alexandro Hernandez handed Greg the stopwatch and joined him at trackside. "She'll be more than ready to start the novice circuit this spring."

Forearms draped over the white rails of the fence bordering the quarter-mile practice track, Greg squinted against a noonday sun as the little blue roan danced and fought the bit at the starting gate. Her coat gleamed. Well-honed muscle quivered.

"You've done a good job with her Alex. Who's on board today?" He nodded toward a rider he didn't recognize.

Alexandro grinned. "It's Ramon."

Greg did a double take then smiled. "Well, I'll be damned if it isn't. When did your little Ramon get so big?"

"He's only little in his mother's eyes." The men exchanged knowing looks. "He turned fifteen in September."

"He could always ride. Let's see what he does with the filly."

Chest puffed with pride, Alexandro gave a signal to the gate man. Thirty seconds later, horse and rider burst out of the gate. Greg set the watch.

As fast as a desert wind, Ramon jockeyed the filly down the quarter-mile track and across the finish line. Greg hit the second button, checked the time. Smiling, he showed it to Alex.

Alex chuckled. "Told you."

"Told me straight, too. She can flat-out fly. The boy's good with her."

"He has the touch, my Ramon."

"Is he on salary?"

"Oh, no, Mr. Hunt. Ramon just rides because he loves it."

"Put him on salary," Greg said firmly but with open friendship when Alexandro looked hesitant. "Hell, a kid's got to have a little pocket money. Looks as if he more than earns the right. No, don't get all waffly on this. If you lived in town he'd probably be working at a grocery store or at the diner for some spending money. Since he doesn't have the opportunity way out here and since, from what I can see, he'll be worth every dime, let's just give him a little incentive."

He clapped a hand on Alexandro's shoulder as they ducked under the rail and walked toward Ramon and the racer. "Work it out with Juanita. We don't want her getting upset and worrying that Ramon will neglect his schoolwork."

"Thank you, Mr. Hunt. That's very generous."

"What it is, is fair," Greg insisted, and approaching the filly, he offered Ramon the praise he was due.

Later, his hands stuffed deep in the pockets of a lightweight denim jacket, Greg ducked into the relative warmth of the barns and took his time inspecting his stock. He'd taken his time doing a lot of things since he'd brought Anna here two days ago. Mostly, he'd taken his time staying away from her. Not that it had done any good. Whether he was holed up in his office, haunting the track, riding the range or keeping the hands up with late-night poker games in the bunkhouse, it was Anna he thought of. Anna, who kept him wandering and wondering exactly where they went from here.

Today, he was determined to shake it off. After joining Alexandro for coffee in the tidy house that he and Juanita and their boys shared south of the main house, he'd wandered back to the barns. He didn't get out to Casa Royale as often as he would like. And he sure as hell didn't make it to as many races as would make him happy. But he surely did enjoy the shadowed quiet and the soft sounds that were intrinsic to a horse barn.

The racers nickered softly as he approached each stall. The soft snuffling as they contented themselves with hay from their mangers, the bubbling giggles—

Giggles?

With narrowed eyes and a soft step, he approached the stall at the far end of the alley. Very quietly, he peered inside—to see two little boys hand-feeding oats to a sloe-eyed brood mare. Since he knew Juanita forbade Tito to be underfoot in the barns unless she or Alexandro were with him, he decided he had a couple of little desperadoes on his hands.

PLAY TIC-TAC-TOE

OR FREE BOOKS AND A GREAT FREE GIFT!

Use this sticker to **PLAY TIC-TAC-TOE.** See instructions inside!

THERE'S NO COST•NO OBLIGATION!

Get **2** books and a fabulous mystery gift! **ABSOLUTELY FREE!**

Turn the page to play!

Play TIC-TAC-TOE and get FREE GIFTS!

HOW TO PLAY:

1. Play the tic-tac-toe scratch-off game at the right for your FREE BOOKS and FREE GIFT!

2. Send back this card and you'll receive TWO brand-new Silhouette Desire® novels. These books have a cover price of $3.75 each in the U.S. and $4.25 each in Canada, but they are yours to keep absolutely free.

3. There's no catch. You're under no obligation to buy anything. We charge nothing — ZERO — for your first shipment. And you don't have to make any minimum number of purchases — not even one!

4. The fact is, thousands of readers enjoy receiving books by mail from the Silhouette Reader Service™ months before they're available in stores. They like the convenience of home delivery, and they love our discount prices!

5. We hope that after receiving your free books you'll want to remain a subscriber. But the choice is yours — to continue or cancel, any time at all! So why not take us up on our invitation, with no risk of any kind. You'll be glad you did!

YOURS FREE — A FABULOUS MYSTERY GIFT!

We can't tell you what it is… but we're sure you'll like it!

A FREE GIFT —

just for playing

TIC-TAC-TOE!

DETACH AND MAIL CARD TODAY!

With a coin, scratch the gold boxes on the tic-tac-toe board. Then remove the "X" sticker from the front and affix it so that you get three X's in a row. This means you can get **TWO FREE** Silhouette Desire® novels and a **FREE MYSTERY GIFT!**

PLAY TIC-TAC-TOE

YES! Please send me the 2 Free books and gift for which I qualify. I understand that I am under no obligation to purchase any books, as explained on the back of this card.

326 SDL CX7U

225 SDL CX7N
(S-D-12/99)

Name:

(PLEASE PRINT CLEARLY)

Address: _____ Apt.#: _____

City: _____ State/Prov.: _____ Zip/Postal Code: _____

Offer limited to one per household and not valid to current Silhouette Desire® subscribers.
All orders subject to approval.

PRINTED IN U.S.A.

The Silhouette Reader Service™ — Here's how it works:

Accepting your 2 free books and gift places you under no obligation to buy anything. You may keep the books and gift and return the shipping statement marked "cancel." If you do not cancel, about a month later we'll send you 6 additional novels and bill you just $3.12 each in the U.S., or $3.49 each in Canada, plus 25¢ delivery per book and applicable taxes if any.* That's the complete price and — compared to the cover price of $3.75 in the U.S. and $4.25 in Canada — it's quite a bargain! You may cancel at any time, but if you choose to continue, every month we'll send you 6 more books, which you may either purchase at the discount price or return to us and cancel your subscription.

*Terms and prices subject to change without notice. Sales tax applicable in N.Y. Canadian residents will be charged applicable provincial taxes and GST.

"Afternoon, gents," Greg said, in his best papa bear voice. "Do your mothers know what you're up to?"

As wiry as a monkey and just as fast, Tito clambered up the side of the stall, hooked his toe in the wire manger, and vaulted over the side. He was making tracks and racing out the barn door before William's eyes had popped back in their sockets.

Belatedly, William shot straight toward the stall door to make his own escape.

"Whoa, there." Greg latched on to the boy's belt when he tried to wedge his way between Greg's widespread legs and out of the stall. "What's the rush?"

The minute he touched him, the little boy froze in his tracks. Stiff as a fence post, he stilled to an extreme military form of attention.

Greg frowned, hunkered down in front of him. He stared at the boy's lowered head, thumbed back his Stetson. Not liking the fear in the boy's stance, he proceeded cautiously.

"You like horses, do you?" What little he could see of the small hands poking out from the sleeves of an oversized sweatshirt were balled into fists at William's sides.

"Yes, sir," he said quietly.

Unaccountably angry that the child felt so cowed by his presence that he couldn't even look at him, Greg curled a finger under his little pointed chin.

Damned if he didn't flinch, then fight the instinct and hold himself yet more erect.

"Do I scare you, son?"

A little Adam's apple bobbed once as he swallowed. "No, sir."

He was scared down to his toenails, Greg realized and

felt a swell of admiration for the effort it took him to hold his ground.

"Well that's good—because you have nothing to fear from me. Okay?"

A pair of summer-blue eyes finally braved a look at his. Greg could see him consider if he could trust him, then reserve judgment until proof or the cavalry arrived.

"Now your mom," Greg said, giving the child time to digest what he'd said, "there's a person to fear."

"Not *my* mom," William said, rushing to her aid.

Greg pulled a face. "You telling me you're not afraid of your own mom? Why I heard tell she ate little boys for breakfast, and those she didn't eat, she gave twenty lashes with a wet noodle every night before she sent them to bed."

The beginning of a smile tugged on the corners of William's mouth. "She doesn't do that."

"She doesn't? Well what does she do then?"

He thought for a moment. "She tells me stories."

"About bad moms who eat little boys and—"

"No," William quickly cut in, his voice stronger, his eyes more involved and just hinting at animation. "She tells me stories about cowboys."

"Cowboys, huh?"

"Yeah. Texas cowboys."

Greg refused to let himself think he had been one of the cowboys in those stories a mother would tell a son—even though something deep inside wanted to believe just the opposite.

"You've pretty much got a thing for cowboys, don't you, bud?"

"Yes, sir. And horses. Cowboys feed their horses."

"Ah. So, you figured if you'd come down to the barns

and feed old Bea here some oats, you just might end up being a cowboy too, huh?"

A charming mix of guilt and hope brightened his big eyes.

Greg thought for a moment, thought better about what he was about to do, then thought, what the hell. The boy wanted to be a cowboy, he could, by God, be a cowboy.

He nodded toward the mare. "How about we saddle her up?"

If possible those enormous eyes grew even bigger. "I could ride her?"

Greg smiled. "Would you like that?"

The boy was so thunderstruck, all he could do was nod.

"Well, come on, then, Wild Bill, let's get this show on the road."

Greg stood and, on instinct, held out his hand. On instinct, the little boy took it.

And something inside Greg warmed and expanded.

William's hand felt small and fragile enclosed in his big palm and callused fingers. Yet it fit. As they walked side by side to the tack room to get a brush and a bridle, Greg couldn't shake the pleasant sensation that it fit just fine.

They had just finished brushing down the mare—Greg on one side, William perched on a step stool on the other—when Anna came racing into the barn, her long hair flying.

"William," she cried in relief when she spotted him.

"I'm going to be a cowboy," he bubbled happily, oblivious to the panic on his mother's face.

Greg was oblivious to nothing. Not the high flush of color on her mottled cheeks. Not the snug fit of her jeans, the delicacy of the hand that reached up to tuck a long strand of pale-gold hair behind the perfect shell of her ear. Not the rise and fall of her breasts beneath the pale blue V-neck sweater that bared the slender column of her throat and revealed the milky whiteness of her skin.

Anna rushed to William's side, then stopped suddenly when she realized that William and Greg appeared to be in league together.

"He's fine, Anna." Greg smiled across Bea's broad back and felt a warmth flood through him when William's answering smile was quick and unguarded. "He understands now that he and Tito should have asked permission before coming down here. They won't be doing it again. Right, Wild Bill?"

"Right." He glanced at his mom, his excitement overriding any attempt at contrition. "We're brushing Bea because a cowboy always has to take care of his mount. And then I'm going to ride her."

Greg was quick to quell the panic on Anna's face. "Bea's nineteen, Anna. She's baby-sat more kids than a day-care center. I'll just lead them around the indoor arena to let Will here, find his seat. Okay with you?"

Very evidently, it wasn't okay. Greg could see it in her eyes, in the way she knit her fingers together until she blocked the blood flow. But it would be her decision, one he would respect. One, when she made it, filled him with a pride over which he had no ownership.

"Do...do you care if I watch?" she asked William. "It's not every day a mom gets to see her very own cowboy make his first ride."

William beamed. Greg gave her a slow smile when what he wanted to do was eliminate her worries with a soft kiss to her furrowed brow. Too aware of the effect she had on him and needing to waylay it, he set down his brush.

"You need to stand back while I saddle her up, okay pardner? You watch, though, so you can learn how to do it yourself someday."

All business, his intelligent blue eyes glued to Greg's every move, William watched without comment or question. Only his shifting feet gave away his building excitement.

"Ready to mount up?"

William's nod was quick and confident. "I'm going to ride like the wind."

Greg chuckled. To his relief, Anna did the same as her excitement for her son overrode her own reservations.

As he helped little William onto the big horse's back and witnessed the child's unbridled happiness and the shimmering pride in his mother's eyes, Greg slid, quite easily, into a decision he hadn't been aware he'd been weighing.

The surprise of it didn't stun him as much as it should have. Neither did it scare him. And he should have been scared. Running scared. Relief, instead, outdistanced any sane reaction. Relief was as sweet as the look on Anna's face, worth every delay of an insight that had been far too long in coming.

He was done fighting. Just like that, he was tossing down the gloves. He was done battling with his feelings, with his doubts, with his anger. Anna was not the cold, calculating aristocrat his bruised pride had painted her to be. She was just a woman. A woman with obligations that ruled her choices. A woman with strong loyalties and an inbred sense of duty.

Yeah, it had hurt like hell that she had let him leave

her four years ago. It had hurt like nothing he had ever experienced before or wanted to experience again. But she hadn't let him go because she hadn't wanted to be with him. He should have realized that four months ago—the moment he'd first seen her. Those expressive green eyes had told him exactly how she felt. Only his pride had refused to let him see it.

She still loved him. She had loved him from the beginning. In fact, she'd let him go because of that love. She'd felt she'd had no choice. Maybe she hadn't. Maybe, he realized, too late, he should have fought harder.

And maybe what should have and could have didn't have any place in what was happening between them now.

What was happening now was, she was here—the Anna he remembered. Kind. Compassionate. Caring. In the smile she had just given up for her son, he saw a glimpse of the young woman he had fallen in love with that European summer. He'd seen a spark of the girl who had loved without reservation, had thrown caution to the wind and given him four of the best days of his life.

That girl was still there. And now, so was the woman. In the kiss they had shared on their wild flight from the media mob, he'd found that woman. The one who melted at his touch. The one who turned him into the man he was only able to be in her arms.

Loving her wasn't an option. It was clear to him now that it had never been an option. Just as it was clear that he'd never stopped caring. He'd just stopped believing.

As he walked the mare around the arena, he accepted that it might not be wise to open himself up to loving her again. But he'd done wise for the past four years. Wise was isolating and lonely. Wise was comprised of short-term, empty relationships and hollow feelings. No, wanting Anna may not be wise. Needing her, however, had become undeniable. And weren't things different now? She was here on his turf. She was here on his terms. And he was past the point of not taking advantage of those sweet, if unholy facts.

William laughed in delight as Greg led him in a slow circle around the arena, then stepped up the pace to a trot. He glanced at Anna as they trotted by, saw the happiness of her heart through her eyes—and that vital, compelling hope, sealed the deal.

She was his. Then. Now. Forever. He'd work it out. Somehow, he'd find a way to work it out.

In the meantime, he would simply let it happen. He would ride on this rich sense of freedom that suddenly swamped him. Enjoy the slow uncoiling of a painful tightness that had grown in the past four years and crowded inside his chest like a loaded spring.

Anna was his. She was his, and this time he wasn't letting her go.

If dawn at Casa Royale was spectacular, that evening Anna learned that dusk could be an event of equal beauty. In the cool soft breeze of early evening, feathery clouds had stacked up on the gray line of the horizon, looming over the endless flatness of the landscape. On its slow descent, the huge orange ball of sun knifed through the breaks of cloud cover in magnificent shades of blue, purple, coral and gold.

Anna had spent four months in Royal. It was a small town, filled with the wonderful flavor of small-town people. She'd met a mix of classes, from the working poor to the Texas equivalent of the socially elite. But what she knew of Texas had been restricted to the city streets, the heat of midday, the city park and the downtown renovation project.

Gregory's ranch, however, represented everything she hadn't seen. Everything she had ever imagined Texas to be. The wide open spaces. The oil wells flanking the access roads. The vastness and the stark, severe beauty of a lost horizon and the biggest sky she'd ever seen.

And now, she'd discovered the most beautiful sunsets in the world. As she sat on a stone bench in the garden, she realized that she'd go through that ugly mob scene at the diner again if even one more day on the ranch was the prize. And having held the prize in her hand, it was going to be that much harder to let it go.

She'd felt attuned to the land from the moment they'd driven out of the city limits and set sail on the relentless wind. Once Harriet had arrived with William, it was as if something that had been out of sync in her life for a very long time clicked quietly into place. Even the nightmares had stopped.

"I believe the line is, penny for your thoughts."

Startled out of her musings, she turned to the sound of Gregory's voice.

He was standing in the shadows. Tall. Strong. Simply watching her—and while it didn't make any sense, she was struck by the notion that he hadn't happened upon her by accident. If that was the case, when he'd seen her, he could have simply turned and left. She never would have known he was there.

He had come out here looking for her. Looking for her, when only yesterday, he couldn't have made a bigger point of always walking away.

When he stepped out of the shadows, her breath caught. When she met eyes that were more pensive than probing, a mouth gentled by the same soft lines he'd

shown William this afternoon, she knew without a doubt
that she was right. He had sought her out.

Some of the tension his presence incited ebbed, then
flowed to an edgy anticipation, a pulsing awareness of
the man and the significance of his actions. Not knowing
how to react to this unexpected development, she braced
her palms on the bench on either side of her hips and
resumed her study of the sky. "I was just thinking how
beautiful it is here."

When he said nothing, she let out a deep breath. Tried
to steady a heartbeat that faltered when he moved nearer.
Nearer. Not farther away.

She braved a look over her shoulder at him, brushing
away a strand of hair the wind had teased into the corner
of her mouth. He had propped a booted foot on the
bench beside her hip, crossed his forearms over his knee
and was sharing her view of the sunset.

"I don't get out here often enough."

She studied the bold lines of his face, shadowed beneath his hat, then offered an opinion on why. "You
work too hard."

He shrugged, his gaze locked comfortably on the horizon. "Maybe."

On the wings of that opinion came a conclusion she'd
been forming since September. "You're very wealthy,
aren't you?"

He angled her a look. Smiled. "Filthy with it."

She thought about that. Thought of the unholy irony.
His blood lines would never be blue, yet he could probably buy and sell her financially insolvent country several times over. A commoner her parents would have
run out of Obersbourg on a gilded, upper-crust rail four
years ago.

The rich colors of dusk ebbed slowly to a velvet darkness as they sat there. But for the undercurrents of something vital, something viable skimming just beneath the surface, the silence was more comforting than uncomfortable.

"I like your Texas," she volunteered finally. Because it was true. Because she felt cocooned in thoughts the silence invited. Dangerous thoughts about what it had been like to make love with him. What it would be like to make love with him again.

"It's so big. The land. The wind. The sky." The people, she added silently. The fact that you are a part of it.

Again, he was quiet for a time. "It's not an easy land. But if a man accepts it for what it is, he'll get along well enough." He angled her a thoughtful look when she turned her face to his. His gaze skimmed from her eyes to her mouth, where it remained.

When he reached out, hooked his little finger on that pesky strand of hair that the wind delighted in teasing, she stopped breathing. When he tucked it gently behind her ear, it was all she could do to keep from leaning into his touch, turning her cheek to his broad, warm palm.

His gaze lingered on hers for the longest of moments before he resumed his study of the sky. "It appears Texas likes you, too."

A fluid warmth flooded her even as his brief touch left her wanting more. She wondered what he saw when he looked at her. She knew what *she* saw. And she liked it. In the few months since she'd been here, she'd put on a little weight—weight she'd needed to steal the gauntness from her cheeks. Her skin had taken on a soft, honeyed tan from even her infrequent encounters with the sun.

Aware, suddenly, of a silence that begged for more

than what either of them could afford to say, she studiously avoided looking his way. "I think maybe it was Manny's cooking…and now Juanita's." She smiled and wished desperately, helplessly that he would kiss her. Then wished she simply could accept that it wasn't going to happen. That it couldn't happen. "If you'd put me anywhere but in a restaurant, both William and I probably would have starved to death."

Something about the stillness had her seeking his eyes again. When she connected with his dark gaze, a shiver that had nothing to do with the night breeze eddied through her body.

"I seem to recall a meal or two you fixed for us once upon a time." His voice was husky, his tone spoke of memories involving more than meals.

Gooseflesh gave way to a flushed warmth, a tingling heat that dovetailed with remembered passion. The memory flowed, instant and vivid: The little second-floor flat with its tiny balcony that he'd rented during his week's leave in Obersbourg. Midnight, candlelight, rumpled sheets…

The sound of Cosmo barking at one of the cats down at the horse barns eased her back to the moment. "Slicing cheese and washing grapes hardly constitutes cooking."

Her words trailed off in a haze of sensation as his gaze caressed and enticed her to remember, just as he was remembering, the sultry friction of skin on skin, the heady taste of wine on his tongue, the juicy, crisp sweetness of the grapes that passed from his mouth to hers.

She turned away, heated by the memory, longing for the reality, as one by one the evening stars pricked the dome of the cobalt sky, glittering in the distance like tiny lanterns strung haphazardly across the heavens.

She searched the night sky, remembering love, engulfed in longing. Waiting, waiting for him to sit down beside her, take her into his arms, tell her how much he wanted her. The connection she felt with him at that moment was so acute, so focused that several thundering heartbeats passed before she realized he was gone.

He'd walked back into the house and left her alone.

Several stunned moments more ticked slowly by before she accepted how badly she didn't want to be alone.

She wanted him back. She wanted him here. And she could have sworn, as they'd shared the intimacy of the night and the magic of memories, that he had wanted her, too.

But wanting, she reminded herself dutifully, had no place in her life. It never had. It never would.

A sudden gust of wind skimmed across her skin, then raced away, inciting a tiny, riotous whirlwind. She watched, in a detached sort of fascination, as it eddied across the garden floor, lifting leaves and scattering them skyward to mingle and dance with stardust before falling in an untidy tumble back to earth again.

Back to earth. Just like she needed to settle her heart back to earth. Back to Texas, where she feared it would stay long after she returned to Obersbourg.

Seven

Greg whistled softly between his teeth as he strolled into the kitchen the next morning. He had risen early, dressed for outside work and headed to the barns. It felt good. Damn good to push something other than paper and corporate competitors' buttons for a change. Hell, it had even felt good to push a broom—which he'd done for a better part of the morning. He'd pitched in and helped clean out the foaling barn in preparation for the colts that would be dropping shortly after the first of the year.

Dusting his hands on his thighs, he sniffed out the pan of warm sticky buns Juanita had cooling on the counter and let a huge grin take over. "Jackpot."

After washing up and pouring a mug of coffee, he snagged a bun, moaned in ecstasy at the first mouth-watering bite and wandered toward the sounds coming from the great room. Great sounds, he decided, leaning a shoulder against the archway to enjoy the view.

The four of them—Juanita, Tito, Anna, and little Will were alternately digging into cardboard storage boxes and making oohing and aahing noises as they dragged out Christmas ornaments and scattered them over furniture and floor.

He held back there for a moment, taking it all in, enjoying the warmth, the sense of celebration. As little as a few days ago, he would have felt separated from the scene, a window-shopper, merely looking in. As of yesterday, however, that sense of exclusion had been obliterated by a longing look, a needful invitation from seeking green eyes as telling as a love song.

It had been hard to walk away from her in the garden last night. It had also been necessary. Absolutely necessary to leave her with stars in her eyes and a wanting in her heart that he strongly suspected echoed his own.

But it had been too soon for her. Too new, this reawakening. She needed time to get used to it. And he, he'd needed time to get it under control. Yeah, he wanted her. Yeah, he'd finally accepted that his feelings ran deep. He wasn't ready to risk scaring her off. So he'd walked away. He'd left her there among the stars. And if he was half the man he needed to be, he'd leave her there again.

Until she was ready.

He polished off the sticky bun and shoved away from the archway. "What's all this?"

Juanita glanced up to see him standing there, then reached deep into a tall box. "Oh, good. You're just in time, Mr. Hunt. We need some help with the wreath."

Greg angled Anna a smile. Caught up in the festive mood, she forgot to guard herself against her feelings and fired one right back at him. When she realized how spontaneous her reaction was, she toned it down, looked away and busied herself with untangling the string of lights draped over her lap.

He knew he was spinning her off course. She was used to his cool reserve. Since yesterday, he'd done a complete about-face—lost the ability to manufacture cold indifference, ditched his determination to avoid eye contact.

"Look," William cried, scrambling to his feet when he spotted Greg. Clutching a brightly colored figurine in his hands, he raced across the room toward him.

"Whoa, cowboy." Snagging the boy just as he tripped over a rope of garland, Greg hauled him onto his hip. "What have you got there?"

"Santa's a cowboy, too. Just like me. Look." William patted a small hand against Greg's cheek to make sure he had his full attention.

Laughing, Greg dutifully inspected the plaster figurine of a rosy-cheeked Santa astride a black-and-white horse. "You think he can ride like the wind, too?"

"Oh, yes. Santa can fly! Him and his reindeer. Do you think Santa's horse can fly, too?"

Greg chuckled and settled the boy more comfortably on his hip. "Well, I don't think Santa would own a horse that didn't fly."

"I don't think so, either."

Anna watched the exchange with a catch in her heart. Seeing the way Greg's eyes drifted in a warm caress over her face contributed to the sensation. It was the sight of father and son together, so completely taken with each other, however, that pulled at strings and tugged on knots she'd been afraid to let unravel.

The exchange made it very clear that Gregory felt

genuine affection for William. Those big, strong hands held him with such gentle care. The sparkle lighting his eyes was spontaneous and honest.

Twin blades of hope and regret sliced her heart. Hope, for the relationship that was budding, healed things inside her that had been wounded for a very long time. Regret, for the years father and son had been separated, ate at her in ways she had never fathomed. And always, guilt overrode it all. She had to tell him. She had to tell him soon.

With a soft pat to his bottom, Greg set William back on the floor where he scooted over to investigate the box that had caused Tito to launch into another chorus of "Oh, man, this is waaay cool."

"I thought I heard somebody say something about a wreath." While he spoke to Juanita, Gregory's attention was fixed on Anna, his smile soft and intimate, his eyes blue and clear.

"This one," Juanita said, giving Anna an excuse to look away from the pull of Gregory's gaze to the huge hoop of pine cones, assorted nuts and a brilliant red ribbon that Juanita lifted from the box. "It goes over the mantel."

"Where did I get all these decorations, Juanita?" Greg asked after he'd left the room then come back with a tall stepladder.

"Oh, you've accumulated them over the years," Juanita said, tongue in cheek. Both knew good and well that she was the one who had seen to it that Casa Royale was dressed for the holidays every year.

"Well, I certainly have excellent taste." He grinned down at her as she handed him the wreath.

"I've always thought so." Juanita's dark eyes snapped with mischief.

"Makes me wonder why I haven't been around to enjoy all my handiwork more over the years."

"Maybe you didn't have a good enough reason to come around more often," she added with a quick, but not altogether sly, look Anna's way.

"Maybe." He hefted the wreath into place and centered it before climbing down the ladder and meeting Anna's eyes again. "Maybe that's exactly the way I see it, too."

Under his considering gaze, Anna blushed. She was dazzled. His warm smiles and velvet looks all but danced as he joined them for the rest of the morning as if he had nothing better to do. He hammered nails. He hung garland. He repaired strings of lights.

Once, he came up behind her while she was standing on a step stool, draping garland over the arch of a window.

"Careful," he whispered, close, so close, as the warmth of his big hand settled proprietorially on her hip. "It wouldn't do to have you lose your balance and fall."

She'd been in no danger of losing her balance. Not until that moment. The touch of his hand on her hip, the gentle puff of his breath tingling at her midriff, just below her breasts, his unique blend of aftershave that made her think of desert nights, of the cinnamon on his breath from Juanita's sticky buns, the lingering and entirely pleasant presence of horse, hay and sunshine—it all hit her in a dizzying rush.

She was in danger then. Of falling. Of sinking into his arms and never coming up for air.

"You okay?" he murmured, his mouth so close to her body, his eyes searching.

For a long, mesmerizing moment she couldn't move. She could only stare, tethered by his gaze, shaken by his touch, wanting, wanting desperately to lean down to him, to close the distance between their mouths and taste the heat of his kisses.

"Anna? Are you all right?" His hand tightened on her hip, his eyes never left her mouth.

A sizzle of response so electric she jolted had her stepping quickly down from the stool. "Fine. I'm fine."

Of course, she wasn't. She was flustered, confused and totally at odds to understand his actions today given the way he'd disappeared from the garden last night.

"Is it time to decorate cookies yet?" Tito's excitement bubbled into the room and broke the spell.

"It's time, it's time," William chanted as Anna ran an unsteady hand over her hair and tried for a settling breath.

"That's my cue to beat a hasty retreat," Gregory said, backing toward the door.

"You have to help!" William cried. "You have to."

It was all Anna could do to keep from crying out, too. She didn't want him to leave, either. Although she knew it wasn't wise, she wanted to experience more of this exciting, attentive Gregory who both tempted and confused her.

While William's plaintive little plea was well on the way to turning the trick, when Juanita tossed in a bribe of another sticky bun, Gregory threw up his hands in surrender.

"Okay. Okay. I can see when I'm outgunned. And outmaneuvered," he added with a laugh.

He was still grinning when the phone rang. And Anna was still charmed by the ease with which he'd consented.

"I'll get it, Juanita." He caught it on the third ring. "Hello."

Still in the process of gathering leftover decorations

and tidying up, Anna didn't immediately tune in to the sudden coldness of Gregory's tone.

Something about the way his words became stilted, blatantly abrupt, made her look his way. Even before he told her, the stormy look on his face left little doubt about who was on the other end of the line.

Her buoyant, expectant mood of moments ago shattered like a precious glass ornament under a carelessly placed foot.

"It's your mother," he said, his face as hard as his voice.

She stared from the concern in his eyes to the phone in his hand. She'd known this time would come. She'd known her mother and father would eventually track her down—just as she'd known she would have no choice but to talk with her mother now.

She rose. Wiped suddenly damp palms on her thighs. "I'm surprised it took her this long to find me."

"You don't have to talk to her." Greg's gaze never left her face.

"Yes." She drew a bracing breath. Held out her hand. "Yes. I do."

He searched her face for a long, probing moment before handing her the receiver. "I'll be in the kitchen if you need me."

She smiled—a silent thanks for his support. Then she prepared for the confrontation to come. With her focus centered on the serenity of the garden just outside the window, she lifted the receiver to her ear.

"Hello, mother."

Anna was in the garden when Gregory found her half an hour later. Cosmo, sweet dog, must have sensed her agitation. He sat by her side, his huge box head resting heavily on her lap as she idly stroked his silky coat.

Gregory didn't say anything. He just walked up and sat down beside her.

"After all these years, you'd think I would get used to it," she said, when both his presence and his silent concern prompted her to share her thoughts aloud with someone who wouldn't judge her. Trusting, instinctively, and without question that Gregory was that someone, she didn't hesitate. "She didn't even ask about William. And, of course, she didn't ask about me."

She filled her hand with Cosmo's soft, floppy ear, watched the water gurgle gently in the fountain.

"Her biggest concern was that they don't think they can keep my absence from Obersbourg under wraps much longer. I'm becoming an embarrassment. Again," she added, thinking back to her mother's exact words.

"It's so like you, Anna. Always thinking of yourself. How long do you think we can convince the press you are in seclusion, mourning for Sara? They are getting restless. It's just like that ugly business with William. We had to lie for you then, too. While you pined around for the rogue who fathered him, we had to endure. We had to make up that dreadful story that the father was killed in a military accident in Egypt right after you had become engaged. You ran then, too. Well, you've run too far this time. And you've gone too far. Your duty is here—although after that shocking incident with Ivan— well, I hope you feel sufficient guilt over that. He was our only hope and you destroyed that, too."

Anna closed her eyes, shook her head, attempted to physically shrug off the sting of her mother's cold, impersonal indictment. "I could actually picture her while she was lecturing me. She'd be appalled if she knew her mouth puckered up when she was angry. And that her spine, always as rigid as the hats she insists on wearing and takes such painstaking pride and time selecting, actually bows with anger.''

She wasn't aware that she'd started smiling. "Sara— Sara used to do the most outrageous imitation of her. She'd sneak into the closet and get into mother's hats. Then she'd parade around the halls, her nose in the air—'' Her voice trailed off and just as she wasn't aware that she'd been smiling, she wasn't aware when that smile softly faded. Nor was she aware that Greg had placed an arm around her shoulders and drawn her close. "I miss Sara so much."

"Tell me about her," he prompted gently—and made it easy to share some of her sister with him, to inadvertently share a little of herself in the process.

"There was a large gap between what Sara wanted for herself and what she was forced to accept. Between what she wanted to be and what she was forced to be, between what she was and what she was expected to be. Everyone wanted a piece of her until the inevitable happened. Emotional loneliness led to creative frustration, frustration to rebellions.'' *Rebellions to death,* remained unspoken, unnecessary.

She shook her head sadly. "I remember one birthday when mother ordered the chef to put the wrong number of candles on her cake. Not out of spite—out of apathy. Mother had simply lost track of how old she was and was too complacent to care enough to get it right.''

Again she paused, remembering. "What attention Sara didn't get from our parents, she got from the press's watchful eye. You don't get used to people looking at you all the time. It's difficult because you didn't choose the attention. You were never given a chance, or the circumstances never allowed you to say, Stop, I want to get out of this…this is not what I wanted.''

Realizing abruptly that she had lapsed into sharing her own sense of frustration, she quickly made corrections.

''Everywhere she went she was mobbed by fans. She once told me she felt as if she was walking a fine line between pinup and princess. She always tried to make trade-offs for some free time, but duty required that her time was everyone else's but hers. Environmental ceremonies, school openings, hospital benefits. She didn't begrudge them, but she needed some private time. She loved to ski. She rarely got the opportunity, and when she did she'd be deluged with reporters.''

The heat of Gregory's big body had slowly seeped through to warm the blood that had chilled to ice from the disturbing memories of her life as a princess—of Sara's life—and the conversation with her mother. The solid support he offered stole the defeating weight of her mother's accusations. The serenity of the garden and the brilliance of the Texas sun, both constant, steady sources of strength she had grown to seek and rely on, combined with Greg's strength to snap her back to the moment. Back to the reality that was now—however temporary that may be.

Thinking of Sara—the best of Sara, a laughing, wickedly daring Sara—made her realize that she didn't just miss her sister. She missed her spirit. It also made her realize that just once in her life, she wanted—no, *needed*—to let her own spirit fly free. And it felt, suddenly, that if she didn't act on that need now, right now, it would never happen at all.

Propelled by an acute need to experience even a little of Sara's adrenaline rush of a life, she abruptly shifted her hips on the bench. Facing Gregory, she impulsively reached out and gripped both of his strong hands in hers. "Take me riding," she said in a rush. "Show me your ranch. Show me the rest of the sky."

Her sudden request surprised him. It also concerned him. She could see both reactions in the slight narrowing of his eyes, in the angle of his head as he searched her face.

"Please." She squeezed his hands tightly in hers, then felt the spirit she so wanted to unleash fly a little higher when he turned the tables and engulfed her hands in the strong grip of his. "Just like William," she said, smiling at the memory, "I want to ride like the wind.

"Show me, Gregory. Show me what that feels like."

After the slightest hesitation, one corner of his beautiful mouth tipped up as he gave in and let himself get caught up in her adventurous mood. "How well do you ride?"

"Well enough to leave you in the dust." Amazed and secretly delighted by her sudden audacity and by the surprise on his face, she laughed softly when he broke into a grin.

"Well…" He rose and tugged her to her feet. "I reckon I'll have to take that as a dare, 'cause around these parts, those are fightin' words, little missy."

She laughed again, a quick, spontaneous, absolutely joyous reaction to his teasing drawl and staged swagger. "Take it any way you want, cowboy. Just take me riding."

It was almost one o'clock when they finally closed the last gate behind them and entered open range. There were the cookies to consider—and the long faces two little boys were bound to wear if Greg and Anna hadn't stayed and helped out with the decorating. Not to mention, a quick lunch and a promise to both William and Tito that Greg would let them ride Bea when he and Anna returned from their ride.

Greg had suspected correctly that Anna was used to riding with English tack. The western saddle she sat astride on Slick Skip, a sweet little four-year-old gelding he'd meant for himself to ride, however, didn't seem to be giving her any trouble.

He, on the other hand, was having plenty of trouble. The kind of trouble that made it hard to keep his mind on the ride. He couldn't shake the impact of her shared confidences about her sister. While he had no doubt she had been talking about Sara, he also had no doubt that Anna had lived every one of those experiences right alongside her sister. It painted a grim picture of two lonely little princesses trying to cope with a world that was not of their making. It painted a graphic account of two lovely young women whose lives belonged to the world and never to themselves. One had rebelled, and now she was dead. One had finally escaped. And her future was still uncertain—at least from her perspective. He, however, had some very definitive ideas on the subject.

No, he hadn't anticipated this resurgence of attraction—of love—that had drawn him to her in the beginning. Hadn't expected to find her every bit as beautiful as she'd been when they'd first met. Hadn't guessed he'd discover a maturity that added dignity, grace and, oddly, a touching vulnerability that the young woman he had fallen in love with had not possessed.

The love she exhibited toward William was both heartwarming and hurtful to watch. The thought crept up on him so abruptly he couldn't stop it. They could have had babies together. Four years ago he had conjured images of forever and family. And children. His and hers.

"Are you coming, slowpoke?"

Her lighthearted words spurred him away from his thoughts and back to the moment—and he got in a little trouble again.

Juanita's borrowed gaucho hat looked saucy and sexy on top of the blond hair that Anna had woven into a tidy French braid. While Juanita's jeans and riding boots had been a little too large for Anna, fifteen-year-old Ramon's had fit her perfectly. Too perfectly, Greg thought as he watched her trim little bottom and slim thighs bouncing along ahead of him.

Greg had taken special care selecting their mounts. He hadn't wanted to overwhelm Anna with one of his fiery racers. Neither had he wanted to undercut her new-found sense of adventure. Jody Rose had seemed the perfect choice for her. She was a solid, soft-mouthed black. She had a sensible head and enough speed to keep things interesting.

Yet when Anna had joined him in the barns, she'd taken one look at Skip—recognized that the sorrel gelding had more fire and more speed—and said, "He's for me."

He had to admit, as Anna cued Skip into a jog-trot, then eased him into a rocking lope, that she knew what she was doing.

He pulled up beside her. "You ride well."

She angled him a look, her smile radiant. "It feels wonderful.

"Are there gopher holes?" she asked a moment later. "Can I run him?"

Greg considered the flat terrain, considered the temperature. It was a fine fifty-five degrees, warm for

December, but cool by Texas standards. The horses could handle a good run.

He nodded to a spot ahead of them. "See that buffalo wallow up there?"

She searched, brows drawn together under the shade of her hat brim. "Buffalo wallow?"

He smiled. "That little gully about a quarter mile ahead."

She followed his gaze. "Yes. I see it."

"Well, don't eat too much of my dust on your way there, cowgirl." With a wicked grin, he cued Jody Rose, then gave her her head.

He heard Anna's delighted squeal behind him and knew she'd kneed Skip into a run, too. Just that fast, the race was on.

Greg had some of the finest quarter racers in the States. As fast as Jody was though, with Greg's extra weight, the only way Jody could hold her own in a race against Skip with a lightweight like Anna aboard was with a little head start. They gave it a good run, but he wasn't surprised when, just shy of the finish line, Anna and Skip flashed into his peripheral vision then edged ahead by a nose.

Radiant, was all Greg could think when Anna pulled up and reined Skip around. She vibrated with energy and excitement. She glowed with both happiness and the honest emotion of competition.

"He's fast," she cried, patting Skip's neck in appreciation for a job well done. "And so strong. I never realized these quarter horses had such power."

"He's bred to run, all right. And you'll never encounter a breed with more heart."

His blood still running hot from the fever of the race, Skip crow-hopped sideways, kicking up dust in his wake. "And here I always thought it was the Thorough-breds who had all the fire." Laughing, Anna expertly gathered Skip and settled him down.

"I'd say you're well matched." Greg liked the way Anna handled the spirited sorrel. Liked even more the way she looked astride the gelding, lean yet lush and buzzing with excitement. Like she'd been four years ago the first time she'd danced in his arms. The first time he'd kissed her. The first time they'd made love.

"Now that you've given me a sound beating," he said, needing badly to divert his thoughts, "what would you like to see?"

"Everything," she said so quickly it made him laugh.

"We're talking twenty thousand acres, here, Anna. I don't think *everything* is an option."

"Twenty thousand?" She looked stunned. Looked around. Laughed. "You could fit most of Obersbourg inside your ranch."

"Well, this is Texas," he drawled, nudging Jody up beside Skip until he and Anna were facing each other beneath the brilliant December sun. "You might have heard. We do things big in these parts."

To make sure she understood how big, and to satisfy a need he'd been nursing for way too long, he cupped her nape in his hand and pulled her close. "And we do things right," he whispered as he lowered his mouth to hers.

Her lips were soft and altogether welcoming as he settled his mouth over hers and ended the waiting with a long deep taste. She was as ready for this as he was. As electric in her yearnings as he was with his greed. She tasted of salt, sex and woman. She yielded for the invasion of his tongue, welcomed the stroke of it at the seam of her lips, the thrust of it as he delved deep.

Heat, heart, total capitulation. That's what he felt when he kissed her. That's what she gave him. That's what he took.

Over and over again he tasted and claimed and let her know he was done pretending there was nothing simmering between them, finished waiting for a reason to make her his. Over and over again, she met his demands, made some of her own, until the needs that mere mouths could satisfy left them hungry and impatient for more.

Eyes closed, his hand still cupping her nape, he pulled away, rested his forehead against hers as they both recovered their breath. Beneath him, Jody grew restless.

"Umm," Anna managed on a breath that sounded as ragged and raw as he felt.

"Yeah." He lifted his head, took in her flushed cheeks, the heavy-lidded passion in her eyes. "Umm."

She smiled then. A slow, crooked, self-conscious and slightly victorious smile that made strange things happen inside his chest. Made other things happen much lower and threatened his capability of continuing the ride.

"We'd better get moving," he said, when he wanted nothing more than to lift her out of that saddle and roll around with her in the Texas dust until they were both blistered by the sun—or by their passion.

Eight

The night breeze was mellow. The starlight, a gentle caress. The mood, as serene as a summer rose. Anna felt anything but mellow, or gentle or serene.

What she felt, as she sat in the garden by the fountain, was an edgy, earthy anticipation. William was sleeping over with Tito. That left her and Gregory alone in the house. She knew he would come to her tonight. And she knew when he did, the waiting and the wanting would finally be over for both of them.

Beneath the golden brilliance of the Texas moon, each moment that passed felt essential. Essential as only a handful of moments in a lifetime were essential, moments in which a vital choice must be made. A choice of either tumbling headlong over the edge into something that wasn't entirely wise or pulling away because it was too dangerous.

Far too often in her life, when it had come time to choose, Anna had opted for safety.

She didn't want to feel safe tonight. She didn't want to be wise. She didn't want to think about obligations, guilt and regret. She wanted to feel free. To flow as reckless as the moonglow that danced across the bubbling waters of the fountain and lent a shimmering effervescence to the night, a heady expectancy to the moments she and Gregory were destined to share.

Her mother would be appalled if she knew that her phone call this afternoon had actually been the catalyst for what was about to happen. The harsh words and layers of guilt had been engineered to bring Anna swiftly back to Obersbourg. To a point, she had been effective. It was at the surface again—the reminder of the duties Anna knew waited for her. To that end, her mother had been successful. In all else, she had failed.

Instead of warning Anna away from what she considered impetuous and embarrassing behavior, she had, unintentionally, given Anna the courage to answer another demand. The demand of her heart. And she had made her see and face up to a truth that had been too long denied. A truth that was difficult but necessary to accept.

Anna understood now that she had allowed herself to become a victim. All of her life, she'd deluded herself into believing otherwise. Into believing that she'd been the dutiful daughter, that she'd been fulfilling her predestined subservient role in life. On the heels of her mother's call, however, she now accepted that there was no other word to describe the life she had endured. It had taken the better part of the afternoon to come to terms with the weight of her discovery. The realization had been numbing, soul searing. The truth of it was both humiliating and healing.

Oddly enough, it had also been empowering and head clearing. What had to have been plain to everyone who knew her was now suddenly, stunningly clear to her, too. She'd been victimized by the cold, callous disregard of her parents. She'd been victimized by their lack of love, by their lack of involvement, by their dominance of both her spirit and her pride.

And what had she done to garner not only their indifference but, often, their cruelty? She, like Sara, had done the unforgivable. They had been born the wrong gender.

She rose, walked to the fountain, let the cool water trickle over her fingers. Let the night breeze settle the sudden pounding of the pulse at her wrist. That she wasn't born a male was her sin. It was also her sentence. Only a legitimate male heir could save Obersbourg's sovereignty and prevent it from being gobbled up by, and subject to, allegiance to a bigger power. She and Sara had been little more than inconveniences as children, the equivalent of chattel as they'd grown older, bargaining tools to promote marriage to royalty and wealth and ultimately to produce a legitimate heir to the Obersbourg throne.

Neither William nor Edward could satisfy the requirements. In her parents' eyes, their own grandchildren were embarrassments, mere bastards, fathered by commoners. Because of their illegitimacy, they were of little use. Of less value.

She hugged her arms around herself to stall a chill that even the relative warmth of the Texas night couldn't override. Because of a simple and singular whim of biology, she had been cast in the role of a victim. Because of her own willingness to let it happen, she had not only perpetuated her parents' unforgivable sins, she'd compounded them. No longer. She would be a victim no more.

She squared her shoulders in determination. From this moment on, she would take what she wanted; she would chance what she had never dared, then she would return to Obersbourg as its princess. And when she returned, she would demand her rightful progression to power.

She was no longer willing to be a pawn for her parents' political aspirations. She would not be bartered in exchange for Obersbourg's sovereignty. She would not be sold to ensure solvency. Instead, she would exercise her own power as a woman, use her mind and her sense for business, her talent for economics that her father had never recognized, let alone sought out.

A horse nickered softly from the barns, the restless sound an echo of her own restlessness and the fact that tonight—this night—there was only one thing of utmost importance that demanded her attention. Not her country. Not her obligations. Not even a need that grew more pressing by the moment to tell Gregory about William.

Tonight she would be selfish. The one and only pressing issue was the man, and only the man, who had suddenly appeared from the shadows, seeking her out in the thickest part of the night.

She turned at the sound of his footsteps on the stone walkway. Stalled the little catch in her breath at the sight of him standing there. Tall. Strong. As vital as the moon. As necessary as her need to draw breath.

Behind him, the house was quiet. Beyond the moment was a promise that all was forgiven, that all love between them was not lost. Between them was only a few feet of darkness that she quickly reduced to inches.

''I've been waiting for you,'' she said boldly.

He stood as still as the night. Only his searching gaze

gave away the yearning that matched her own. "And I've been waiting for you…for four years too long."

She touched her hands to the breadth of his chest. "I know. I'm so sorry."

He covered her hands with his, lifted them to his mouth, pressed them to his lips. "Don't be sorry. Not tonight. Just be with me."

She burrowed into his arms, loving him, thanking him. For the gift of his forgiveness. For understanding, at least in this moment, that she could neither offer nor promise more than this one night.

He held her against him as he had one summer that now seemed so long ago. He held her in a way that made her feel fragile yet powerful, intensely feminine, shockingly sensual. Then slowly, he began to move, easing her into a dreamy dance made up of intimate turns, heady sensations—the delicious brush of hip to belly, the tingling glide of thigh meeting thigh, the exquisite friction of breast crushed to chest, the feathery warmth of his breath at her brow.

They didn't need music. They both remembered this dance. Remembered the steps. Remembered the swirling, dizzying sensation of falling into the sweetest heat, the most perfect love.

Beneath the stars, silver shadows fell. Beneath the moon, two lovers—lost so long to each other—kissed. Slow, unhurried, predestined.

"Make love to me," she murmured even as he swept her up and into his arms.

Like the rest of the house, Gregory's bedroom was big, bold, beautiful. Like him. Shadowed by night, the muted colors and high ceilinged walls were illuminated by a low burning fire in the adobe-and-limestone fire-place.

Anna noticed it all on a peripheral level as Gregory carried her inside and set her on her feet beside his bed. It was a big bed. A tall, massive four-poster, hand-hewn of bleached cypress and covered by a thick, downy cream and tawny comforter. No sight had ever looked as welcoming—except for the man who stood before her.

His eyes never left her face as he reached for her, his big hands and blunt-tipped fingers slowly and none too steadily undoing her blouse, one button at a time. She covered his hands with hers, gently guiding, mostly riding with the rhythm, savoring the anticipation and the need and the promise of skin on skin.

The back of a knuckle accidentally grazed her nipple. When she bit her lower lip and softly moaned, he revisited that ultra sensitive area again, this time, no accident, this time to entice, arouse and elevate her need by slow, hot degrees.

He stepped back then, mere inches, and left her wanting, left her weak.

"Take it off," he ordered gruffly when her blouse lay open to reveal the delicate white lace of her bra, the fire-kissed expanse of bare skin.

Never more aware of her need for him, she tugged the blouse from her jeans, shrugged it off, one shoulder at a time, fascinated as he pulled off his boots, then went to work on his own shirt. Unbuttoning then tugging loose his shirttail was as far as he got before he reached for her again, drew her hard against him and into a deep, searing kiss.

The heat was wonderful, the breadth of his big cal-lused hands on her bare back a heady abrasion, a welcome possession. And his mouth…his mouth claimed, commanded, devoured first her lips, then the column of her throat in hungry, biting kisses. She arched to his ravenous onslaught, cried out when he lifted her from her feet, then deposited her on her knees on the edge of the bed.

With his hands spanning her ribs, he drew her to him as he bent his head to her lace covered breast and suckled her through her bra, scraped his teeth in tender abrasion over her sensitized nipple. It was too much—yet not enough—as both of them reached for the clasp of her bra at the same time and fumbled frantically to undo it.

When he swore in frustration, she cradled his head in her hands, laughed softly, surprising him, calming him, steadying him long enough to free her. And then it was nothing but heat on heat. Warm, wet, consuming heat— and she wasn't laughing any longer.

She was dying. The sweetest, most erotic, most sensual death. She buried her hands in his hair as he licked. Arched, breathless for more as he suckled. Cried his name when he bit, then soothed with a lush swirl of his tongue, a nuzzling caress that increased the ache, intensified the burn.

She was still whimpering his name when he laid her back on his bed. Covering her with his big body, he clasped her hands in his, lifted them above her head and pressed her into the mattress with his weight.

The length of him, the heat of him, the need in him— how she'd missed it. How she'd missed this. This vital, brutal strength that hovered dangerously near the surface of his desire for her and that he kept in check by sheer will.

She caught her breath on a throaty hitch when he

kneed her thighs apart. Wrapping her legs around him, she rode with the thrusting rhythm he set, begged him, "Please, please come inside me."

He scattered kisses to her brow, enticed her higher with the gentle, riding motion of his hips. "Soon." He whispered the promise against her parted lips as he reached between them, flipped the snap on her jeans and eased the zipper down. "I want to savor this. I want to remember this."

She sucked in her breath, abdominal muscles contracting to make room for his heated invasion as he slipped his fingers inside, restlessly made do with a teasing touch when what she wanted was all of him, thrusting deep.

He uttered a low, pleasured sound when his fingers encountered her downy softness. Blue eyes bore into hers as he cupped her intimately, then he covered her mouth with his and swallowed her shimmery sigh when he delved deep into liquid heat. She was so ready for him. Wet and swollen. Slick and sweet.

She clenched and moved against the steady pressure of his fingers, and suddenly, his promise of soon wasn't fast enough for either of them. Still half leaning over her, he jerkily shrugged his shirt from his shoulders, then rolled to his back and rid himself of the rest of his clothes and rolled on protection. She was already reaching for him as he tugged her jeans and panties down her hips and clear of her legs. Her small hands sought, her delicate fingers surrounded, making him burn, making her bold as she pulled him back on top of her, where they both knew he belonged.

The first touch of steely male heat to giving feminine warmth stole their breaths. The delicious press, the enticing thrust of man seeking woman, of woman gloving man sent heart rates soaring.

She moaned his name. Let her eyes drift shut on a long, slow surge of sensation as he entered her.

"Look at me," he told her, easing up on his elbows and cradling her head in his hands. "Look at me when I come inside you."

With a slumberous sigh, she obeyed. With a shudder of longing fulfilled, she let her hands drift, fingers splayed wide down the length of his back, then lower, to cup and encourage the driving ebb and flow of his hips.

And all the while, she boldly held his stormy gaze, watched building passion cloud liquid blue eyes to a smoky cobalt, watched studied concentration lose out to a wildly savage plunge into the dark, animal side of desire.

For a desperate moment, she clung to that part of herself that he demanded she give over to his keeping. But only for a moment. Helpless to deny him, she willingly let go and joined him in a wild free fall as he filled her with his heat and his soul, and tumbled them, heart to beating heart, over that dangerous, glorious edge of oblivion.

A gentle beacon of moonlight fell through the tall arch of west windows, illuminating the bed and the beauty lying beside him on tangled sheets.

Greg lay on his side, his head propped on one palm, watching her sleep, watching her stir as he spread his fingers wide over the shallow concave of her belly. Her skin was silk. He couldn't get enough of the feel of it. The fluid heat, the resilient softness.

She stretched like a cat under his caress, lifting her arms above her head, an unconsciously seductive motion that thrust the rosy pink tips of her breasts toward him in an irresistible invitation. Even though he'd had her less than an hour ago, his sex stirred, his hand reached to cover the beautifully quivering tip of her nipple. Instantly, she pebbled against his palm. Deliciously, she murmured her appreciation of his touch.

"I'd forgotten how utterly sensitive and responsive you are," he whispered, watching her breast as he massaged it with his hand, shaped it to his pleasure, teased the turgid nipple with the gentle abrasion of his thumbnail.

She rolled into his caress, totally uninhibited, completely committed to the pleasure he gave, to the pleasure he took. "I've never forgotten how it feels to have you touch me."

He lowered his mouth to her breast, blew softly, then flicked with the tip of his tongue. "Like this?"

She shivered. "Yes."

"And this?" He lifted her breast in the cup of his palm, took her into his mouth, feasted, then slowly slid his broad hand down her torso.

"Oh, yes."

He lingered for a moment at her hip point before delving between the vee of her thighs to separate, probe then finesse her most sensitive flesh to throbbing wetness.

He felt her whole body tense, lifted his head to see her fingers wrap around the spindles in the headboard as she rode with his caress, rocked with the rhythm.

"More?" he murmured lowering his mouth to the underside of her breast, then her belly, nuzzling, gently biting, intentionally tantalizing as he pressed a string of kisses to the inside of her thigh.

"Yes. Oh, please..." she managed on a thready

breath as he moved between her legs and possessed her most vulnerable flesh with his mouth.

Until she moaned.

Until she writhed.

Until she helplessly whimpered his name and he lost his mind for the taste, the heat and the need to be one with her.

Breathing hard, needing her now, he rose to his knees above her, spread his thighs wide and dragged her, as weak as a rag doll, up to meet him. He lifted her until she was straddling his lap. Then he lowered her onto his heat and felt the fever swamp him. With her hands desperately gripping his shoulders and his fingers digging into her hips, he lifted her again, then lowered her with a swift, shattering penetration.

She let her head fall back on a moan. Tangled blond hair trailed down her back like a fall of shimmering gold as she gripped him deep inside and cried his name. On a ragged breath, he swore hers and set a rhythm as wild as a Texas dust storm, as elemental as life, as essential as the relentless beat of their hearts.

Wanton and lush, she poured over him, met him plunge for plunge, rode him stroke for stroke, then shattered in his arms as she peaked again and again, crying out in delirious accompaniment to his ragged breaths and gasping climax.

When it was over, she cried. Huge, wracking sobs of elation, exhaustion, of a frightening and dizzying sensation that the responses he could wring from her threatened a complete loss of self.

Her raw whisper eddied across the sheen of perspiration beading his shoulder as he cradled her against him, his hand knotted in the tangle of her hair. "Too much. I need...I need you too much."

"Not enough," he countered gruffly as he eased them down onto the bed and gathered her close to his side. "Never enough," he murmured against her hair and wondered why, even in the face of the love they had shared, even as he held her in his arms, he felt a hollow, foreshadowing sense of loss.

Anna awoke alone. Not even Gregory's warmth remained in the bedclothes. But his scent lingered. The scent they had made making love. She curled herself around his pillow, feeling a delicious soreness in her limbs, a decadent sense of satisfaction and, unbelievably, an ache for the want of making love with him again.

She'd made a decision as she'd drifted off to sleep before dawn. Nothing was going to compromise this new intimacy they had rediscovered. Not yet. Four years ago, her four short days and nights with him had been the happiest of her life. It didn't seem so much to ask for four more. Just four more days of loving him, of being loved by him, before she risked losing him again, as she feared she would when she told him the truth about William.

After seeing them together, she had little concern about Gregory embracing William as his own. How he would react to what she had done, however, gave her heart-clenching moments of doubt. She had kept father from son, son from father. Was there any explanation, no matter how valid, that could bring back the lost years? Was there any excuse that could justify what both had lost?

Her reasons had been compelling. Her sacrifice great. But would Gregory see it that way? Would any man be able to set aside pride, outrage and honor and forgive her for what she had taken from him?

Soon enough, she would have her answers. But not today. A few more days. It wasn't all she wanted. It wasn't all she needed. But it would be enough to see her through the rest of her life if she were forced to live it without the only man she had ever loved.

Greg had left her sleeping. He'd left her with reluctance. But despite the fact that they had stayed awake most of the night making love, he'd left her in his bed with a surge of energy unlike any he'd known. And he'd felt charged with the Christmas spirit.

Anna didn't know it but the press had not relented. They prowled the perimeters of Casa Royale like the coyotes who roamed the range, lurking predators who waited to feed on whatever scrap of cast-off information they could ferret out with their telescopic lenses. Greg made sure that distant pictures were all they got, stationing men he trusted to keep Anna's confidence at every entrance. Daily, they turned back, and sometimes strong-armed, overachievers into leaving—peacefully or otherwise. Until they gave up or some other story beat out that of "The Princess and the Lone Star Prince," as they had taken to calling the two of them, it wasn't safe taking Anna or William off the ranch.

He, however, was on a mission. To avoid being recognized, he borrowed Alexandro's truck and hat. Then he successfully sneaked past the paparazzi. After making some phone calls from his cell phone on this quick, unplanned trip to Midland, he finished his business there in record time and made it back to Casa Royale, loaded down with packages by late afternoon.

She was waiting for him—as he could only now admit, he had imagined her waiting. In his home. Rushing into his arms, both of them oblivious to Juanita's secret smile as she turned her back and returned to the kitchen.

He barely beat the arrival of the truck bearing the huge Christmas tree he'd ordered on his way to town that morning.

"Whoa!" Tito exclaimed, as he and William came tearing out into the drive, William screeching to a halt, his small feet lost in a pair of scuffed and scarred cowboy boots that Tito had outgrown. "Look at that tree!"

"Yeah. Whoa," William mimicked, as he had taken to mimicking everything his hero, the older, wiser, five-year-old Tito said and did. Clearly though, William didn't know whether to be more awed by the size of the tree or by the crane truck that had brought it.

"What have you done?" Anna asked, her eyes dancing in delighted amazement of Greg's indulgence as yet another truck pulled in behind the first one with a pair of smaller, eight-foot blue spruces aboard.

The boys went ballistic when they saw it. Greg loved every minute of it. Right down to helping set up each of the smaller trees—one in Alexandro and Juanita's family room and one in the great room of the main house. The third tree, the largest, was positioned in a sheltered corner of the garden, where anyone at Casa Royale who passed within ten yards could see it trembling in the breeze, hundreds of lights blazing.

"It's all very beautiful," Anna said later, after Juanita and Tito had gone home and William had fallen asleep, worn out from tossing tinsel and sitting on Greg's shoulders to drape garland and hang ornaments. "You didn't have to go to such trouble."

He pulled her closer to his side where they sat on the plush sofa, doing some indulging of his own in the classic brilliance of the beautifully decorated tree. "I enjoyed it,'' he said, matter-of-factly. "It was fun. Made me feel like a kid again.''

She angled her head around to look at him. "You have good family memories.'' It wasn't a question as much as it was a conclusion that appeared to please her.

"The best.''

"I'm glad.'' She laid her head back on his shoulder and snuggled, staring peacefully at the glittering tree. "And now William will have some, too.''

Greg's mellow mood was shattered by a sharp and edgy unease. Unease intensified to anger as he digested not so much what she had said as what she hadn't. William had no good memories of Christmas. None except those that he was sure Anna had tried to make for him.

And what, he wondered, resting his chin thoughtfully on top of her head and staring, unseeing, at the tree, had Anna and Sara endured?

Nine

Because the press kept their vulture's vigil at numerous points along the heavily guarded ranch entrances, Greg called in some family markers and convinced everyone that the Hunt family Christmas celebration should take place at Casa Royale this year. In truth, it hadn't taken much effort. Everyone was concerned about Anna and William—and curious about Greg's protectiveness and attention toward the princess and her son.

Juanita was beside herself with excitement over the prospect of cooking for the entire family—which included the extended families of everyone living and working at Casa Royale and any relatives they chose to invite. Anna was ecstatic over the impending arrival of the twins and Josie and Blake, and visibly nervous about how Gregory's parents would feel about her and William's imposition on their son's life.

"My father quit questioning what I do and why I do

things long ago. And my mother—my mother is a typical mother. As long as I don't break any laws, and it makes me happy, she thinks everything I do is perfect.''

She hugged him hard and smiled up into his eyes. ''How lucky you are to have such a wonderful family.''

Greg touched a thumb to her cheek, gently ran it down to her jaw. She'd never again mentioned the phone call from her mother. Some stories, however, were revealed without the telling. And what little she'd shared with him about Sara had given him a wealth of insight into what had gone on in that stone-cold palace when she was a child. He wished desperately that he could make up to her the good memories she didn't have and that he had taken for granted.

''You say that about my family now,'' he said with a chuckle and every intention of building good memories for her from this day on. ''But you haven't encountered the entire clan together under one roof.''

And under one roof, Anna was soon to find out, the Hunt men and their women were a delightful experience.

Christmas Day dawned clear and unseasonably warm. Only the whupp, whupp, whupp of the chopper blades that heralded the arrival, by helicopter, of Gregory's family matched the thunderous beat of Anna's heart.

She waited in the garden until the chopper touched down and the blinding whirlwind stirred up by the rotor blades settled. Nervously, she ran a hand over her hair, then checked her reflection in the patio windows. Gregory had given her a gift last night when they'd celebrated Christmas Eve together. The pants and tunic were tailored from raw silk, a subtle shade of marbled jade.

''Like your eyes,'' he'd said when she'd opened the gift. ''I'm tired of seeing you in hand-me-down jeans. When things settle down, we'll have to remedy that.''

When things settle down. His words had stayed with her long after William, exhausted by the excitement of Santa's long-awaited arrival, had fallen asleep. Long after the two of them had made sweet love and she'd drifted into a restless slumber haunted with doubts about the possibility of things ever settling down—not in the way he meant.

Not wanting to spoil the day with the threat of what tomorrow or the next day could bring, and unable to stand the waiting any longer, Anna rushed outside and hurried across the fifty yards that separated the heliport from the house. The sight of Josie stepping down out of the copter, little Edward in her arms, brought happy tears to her eyes. Blake followed and helped his mother to the ground, baby Miranda sleeping comfortably against her shoulder.

"Anna!" Josie hurried toward her. "Oh, it's so good to see you." She laughingly transferred Edward into Anna's arms after they embraced. "You look good. You look—happy," she finally concluded with a considering and satisfied grin.

Gregory's mother, Janine, joined the two women, all smiles as she turned a sleeping Miranda in her arms for Anna to see. "Hello again, my dear. And Merry Christmas."

Gregory's father, Carson, echoed his wife's sentiments. "So when do we eat?"

The lot of them laughed, including the pilot, who turned out to be Lawrence, the owner of the very proper voice belonging to the overseer of Gregory's Pine Valley mansion. They all trooped toward the house, where Juanita, Alexandro and Ramon waited by the door, their hands full corralling an excited William and Tito, who were wild to get closer to the chopper and the dangerous rotor blades.

"This was a wonderful idea, Gregory," Janine volunteered as they entered the garden. She smiled and gave him a speculative look when she saw the mammoth tree glittering in the sunlight. "It's been too long since we've made the trip to Casa Royale."

Her animated face momentarily closed like a shuttered window when she spotted William. She stopped abruptly, then recovered. Smiling at William, she transferred the still sleeping Miranda into Blake's arms. "And who, may I ask, is this attractive young man?" Her eyes were alight with warmth and curiosity.

"This is Wild Bill—William to his mother," Greg volunteered, absently touching a hand to William's dark hair.

"William, is it?" Janine said softly. Her gaze left the little boy's face for a mere moment to connect briefly with Anna's, then Greg's. "Well, you are a handsome one, aren't you?" She touched a gentle and lingering hand to his cheek before manufacturing a huge smile and turning the full effect on Tito and Ramon. "And you two, my goodness how you've grown. Big and strong like your father. As handsome as your mother."

"Merry Christmas, Mr. and Mrs. Hunt," Alexandro and Juanita said in unison, accepting the older woman's warm embrace.

"Everything smells wonderful, Juanita." Janine strode briskly toward the kitchen. "Now what do you need me to do?"

Without another word, she disappeared through the great arch toward the delicious aromas of a full-blown Christmas feast—leaving Anna wondering, and worrying, if Janine Hunt's eyes were as wise as they appeared to be.

It turned out there were twenty-five for dinner. Alexandro's parents and his brother and his wife made the drive from Odessa. Several of the hands, loners either by choice or circumstance, shyly joined the festivities. They ate, drank wine and acted properly surprised when Santa arrived by horseback, looking suspiciously like Alexandro, who had slipped down to the barns on the pretense of checking on the horses.

There were presents for everyone—but the most treasured of all were the shiny new cowboy boots that fit William perfectly and looked terrific with the brand-new hat Gregory had given him Christmas Eve.

The dishes were long cleaned up and twilight was approaching when Anna wandered out to the garden for a moment alone.

"It was a lovely day," Janine said, walking quietly up behind her.

Anna turned at the sound of her voice to meet eyes of a clear, stunning blue, so like Gregory's.

"It was very generous of you to share it with us," she said, knowing, with a catch in her heart that their meeting here was not accidental.

"And what do you have to share with me, child?" Janine asked with a directness that even her soft Texas drawl couldn't diminish.

There was nowhere to look. Nowhere to hide. And yet Anna couldn't find the words she knew she must confess. She'd seen Janine's face the moment she had set eyes on William. Her question confirmed that Janine had known then what only a mother knows, what only a mother could have realized in that split second of recognition.

When Anna said nothing, Janine sat down beside her on the stone bench by the fountain. "Have you told Gregory?"

Anna searched the woman's face for anger, or disgust, grateful and confused when she found none, yet still unable to answer her.

"He looks..." Janine said quietly before her voice broke. Her eyes misted. "He looks exactly like Gregory when he was that age." She drew a deep breath, composed herself, then met Anna's gaze. "I need to know if you've told my son yet," she pressed with gentle but firm determination.

Anna physically felt the longing in Janine's voice. Weighted by a guilt that crushed like a vise, she shook her head, ashamed.

"But you will." There was steel in Janine's voice, cloaked in velvet, cushioned by compassion, but steel, nonetheless. "Or I will," Janine assured her, as only a mother who loves her child could.

"You must hate me."

Janine was silent for a long moment. "I would find it difficult to hate the woman my son is in love with."

Anna lifted her head.

"Yes, dear. I know my son. He loves you. And he's already half in love with William."

Anna closed her eyes as the pain closed in.

"Tell him," Janine insisted. "If your reasons are compelling, he will forgive you. And so will I." After a long pause, she touched a hand to Anna's, a hand that trembled as much as her own. "Please make it soon. I want to know my grandson. I want him to know me and his grandfather."

She left her then. Left her knowing, as she had always
known, what she had to do. Understanding, as she never
had, that she could put off the inevitable no longer. Accepting, yet still desperate to deny, that when she told
Gregory, she risked losing everything.

The chopper lifted off like a Texas whirlwind, all
riotous sound and swirling dust. Behind, it left a star-
studded sky. Beneath the sky stood a man who felt he
had everything in life he could possibly want—except
for the formality of a commitment from the woman he
loved. The woman who, unaccountably, looked so lost
when what he wanted for her was to feel found. By love.
By family. By their future together.

"I told you they were overwhelming," he whispered,
turning her into his arms and holding her, just holding
her close. "Blake wore Will out. He dropped like a stone
an hour ago."

"He was wonderful with him. They were all wonderful. They *are* wonderful," she murmured against his
chest as her arms twined around his waist and she burrowed close.

"They think you're pretty special, too."

A deep, weary breath was her only response.

He ran his hands up and down her back, needing more
from her, letting her know with the brush of his lips to
her brow. "So do I. I think you're very special.
Anna…" He cupped her head in his hands, tipped her
face to his and, in the moonlight, saw the moisture clinging to her lashes. "Baby. What? Tell me what's wrong."

Those misty green eyes searched his with such urgency, then demanded with such greed. "Make love to
me. Make love to me." She plunged her fingers into his

hair and pulled his mouth down to hers. "I need you…so much…so much…right now."

And her need, her need, became his, as she took his mouth with hers, dragged him under with her hunger, pulled him deep into the flash fire her passion sparked.

He was lost to resist her. Swept up in the rush of the ride. Somehow they managed to stumble into the house still knotted in each other's arms, mouths fused, hearts wildly beating. They fell on his bed together, tugging on zippers, shoving at clothes, finally gorging themselves with the thrilling feel of skin on skin, heat on heat.

She was wild for his touch on her body, made him wild in return. She was mad for the length of him, the thickness and the heat of him…in her hands…in her mouth. Moaning her name, devastated by her glorious torture, he lifted her above him, his hands moving from slender shoulder to silken hip as he impaled himself inside her, driving deep.

And then he let her have her way with him. She took all of him in, let him fill her completely, then set the pace, a hard, frenzied coupling that demanded and commanded all that he had to give, all that she wanted to take. He gave until they were both exhausted; he gave until they were both quivering masses of spent flesh and hammering heartbeats. Heartbeats bursting with a desperate love that only this rough and ragged mating could assuage.

On a shimmering sigh, she stilled above him, her climax arching her back, wringing out a moan, as she clenched him within her body and rode on the swells of a savage release. Her orgasm flowed through him, wound around him, robbing him of the strength to stay the pleasure any longer.

"Anna," he breathed on a strangled groan as he gave

over to the need, spilling his seed inside her body and
his soul into the liquid depths of her eyes.

The Texas moon peeked through the bedroom windows, floating like a translucent magician's globe suspended on the inky backdrop of a star-speckled sky.
Anna knew Gregory was awake beside her. She sensed
the wakeful rhythm of his breathing even before his big,
gentle hand began an absent, stroking caress along the
length of her thigh.

"You okay?" he whispered, his breath falling softly
against her brow.

She stared into the night. And prayed it wasn't their
last one together. "I'm okay."

He was silent for a while before he rose up on an
elbow and looked down at her. The moonglow high-
lighted his strong profile, lent an aching vulnerability to
the bold lines of his face. The face that she loved more
than life.

"Is it William's father?" he asked so softly but so
abruptly that she felt herself flinch before she could stall
it.

"Is that what this is about, Anna? I've felt you pulling
away since my parents arrived. I've seen your heart ache
through your eyes. And I've wondered...I've wondered
if you're missing him. If you're loving him still and
wishing it was him, not me asking you to share his life."

Above the pounding of her heart in her ears, she heard
the pain in his voice. A pain she had no choice but to
increase. A pain she could no longer forestall. The opportunity was here. The window had sprung up before
her, and it was Gregory who had unwittingly opened it.

She shifted away from him, felt the loss of his heat,
sensed the hurt in his eyes. Bracing for what was about

to happen, she pulled the sheet up over her breasts, drew a deep breath and prepared herself to begin the end.

"When I found out I was pregnant," she began, hardly recognizing her voice as her own as the words echoed hauntingly off the walls in the room where she lay. With the man she loved. With the man she would lose. "When I found I was pregnant, my parents were furious. They made threats."

His big body tensed beside hers. "Threats?"

"Threats that…well, it's hard to explain, hard for anyone to understand. They are powerful people. And they are heartless. I don't think anyone could understand how frightened I was, how badly I wanted to contact…to contact William's father."

She braved a look at him then, saw the veiled disappointment in his eyes and pressed on. "But I was afraid. For the baby. For him. For what they could do to him," she stated, hearing the ominous ring in her words. "They could have done things, Gregory. Arranged things. They wanted his name. I wouldn't tell them. If they'd known…if they'd known who he was, they would have stopped at nothing to ruin him. At least I was convinced of it at the time."

She paused, reflecting, searching even now for some way all this pain could have been avoided. She hadn't known then that Gregory was a man of wealth. To her, he was her marine, her free-spirited working man. To her parents, he would have been a lowly commoner they would have crushed beneath the heels of their outrage. But she hadn't known he'd had the means to fight back, not until she stumbled onto that article in *Newsweek* last year. Hadn't known his family was as high profile in Texas as hers was in Europe.

A cold dose of reality swamped her, stole her doubts

and cemented the inevitability of the choices she'd had
to make.

She'd never expected to see him again, had been too
frightened for him to ask for his help when she'd found
out she carried his child a few months after he'd left
Obersbourg. And she'd been certain that she had destroyed whatever love he may have had for her when,
for his sake, she had convinced him she didn't love him.
For his sake.

"They arranged for an abortion," she hurried on,
swallowing back the memories, scurrying to keep ahead
of the doubts. "When I found out, I ran. When they
finally found me, thankfully it was too late. So they
changed tack—threatened to take William away from me
as soon as he was born."

A rueful smile tilted one corner of her mouth. "Appearances are everything to my parents. And that fact
was my only defense against them. I convinced them
that I would reveal my 'indiscretion,' as they referred to
it, to the entire world if they took William away from
me. The humiliation would have killed them. I must
have been convincing, because they finally just left me
alone. They saved face by fabricating a story and feeding
it to the media. They said that I'd been secretly engaged
and was about to marry a high-ranking officer in the
Obersbourg army who had tragically died during military maneuvers in Egypt. It didn't give William legiti-
macy, but it gave him respectability and a sympathy factor that overrode any scandal."

In the dark, only the sound of his breath, no longer
even, but forced and deep, diluted the silence.

"You shouldn't have gone through this alone.
He…William's father should have been there for you."

She turned to him then, her vision blurred by tears she

could no longer stall. "He couldn't be there. He didn't know. If he'd known, he would have tried to move heaven and earth to get to me. And he would have been destroyed in the process."

"So you protected him and sacrificed yourself."

"I felt I had no choice."

"You had so little faith in him?"

Again, silence crowded into the bed, into her head, compelling her to finally disclose her secret. "I had every faith in him. I loved him. I loved him so much, I didn't want to cause him pain.

"I love him still," she confessed, her voice raw, her heart riding on the wings of that truth, sinking in the waves of despair as she touched her palm to his cheek and turned his face to hers. "And it seems that in spite of it all, I've ended up hurting him more than any man should be hurt.

"I'm so sorry, Gregory. I'm so sorry I had to keep William from you."

She saw the moment confusion turned to understanding, understanding to stunned shock, shock to an anger so huge and anguish driven that he threw back the covers and bolted up in one swift, involuntary motion.

He stood naked by the bed, towering over her, tension coiled like knots in every sleek, honed muscle. "William…William is mine?" Hope jockeyed with disbelief, hurt wrestled with elation, and all transitioned to a look of such bleak, stark betrayal she could only nod and watch him look away. Watch him rake his hands roughly through his hair. Watch him walk, tall and slim and strong, out of the room. Watch him leave her alone with an ache so huge she felt dwarfed by the size of it.

So this is it, she accepted rising slowly from the bed they had shared. She gathered her clothes like an autom-

aton as she moved from the room. She didn't have to
look far to find Gregory. The soft glow from the night-
light by William's bed silhouetted his broad shoulders.
He stood as still as a statue. As rigid as an oak. Watching
over his son. Watching over the son he had been denied.

Without a word, she turned, walked silently back
down the hall and into the guest bedroom. And there she
stayed. Alone. Awake. Conditioning herself to accepting
that she had just lost everything essential in her life.

Somewhere around dawn, Greg left William's side,
dressed in riding clothes and headed for the barns. Like
a distant echo of a truth he should have known, a secret
she'd had no right to keep, Anna's words replayed over
and over in Greg's mind.

A son. My God, he had a son.

As he saddled Skip, he still felt mired in a quagmire
of emotions. Shock. Elation. Love for William. Such
love for William.

And Anna. God help him, he no longer knew what he
felt for her. He'd been ready to ask her to marry him.
But this…this bludgeoning sense of betrayal just kept
hammering away.

Slipping a gate latch, he swung into the saddle and
headed for the open range. And then he rode. And rode,
not willing to admit that he was trying to outrun his
anger and his pain.

She'd had no right. Damn her, she'd had no right to
keep him from his son. She'd had no right to assume
she was protecting him.

"Protecting me," he roared aloud, sending Skip into
a skittish dance that nearly tossed him from the saddle.

She hadn't trusted him. Hadn't believed in him.

Hadn't turned to him. And that sorry truth hurt more than anything she could have done. Anything except losing this time with William.

The overwhelming sense of loss underscored his anger, overrode his love in a consuming grief for the years he had lost, and escalated to a bone-deep rage.

Abruptly, he reined Skip around, headed back to the house at a fast run.

He found Anna in the garden. Looking pale. Looking wounded. Looking like a woman who knew guilt like no other.

"Why now?" he demanded, knowing he was lording over her, inviting her to cower, hating himself as much as he wanted to hate her for blowing a hole through his heart. "Why are you telling me this now?"

"Because you deserve to know. Because William deserves to know. He deserves to know you."

"And I didn't deserve to know four years ago? Four years, Anna. You stole them from me. You stole them from him."

Anna met the wounded eyes of the man she loved and accepted that he was no longer the same man who had professed his love for her. This was an angry man. Righteously angry. Distant and confused. He was asking questions, but she understood that he didn't really want to hear her answers. He wanted her to hurt. He wanted revenge. And she knew he was entitled.

So she didn't try to justify what she'd done. What she did offer was the reason why, after all these years, she'd felt compelled to turn to him.

"I wouldn't have been able to stall Ivan," she said without preamble. "He was devious. He was determined to increase the size of his holdings by marrying me and merging Asterland with Obersbourg. I would have survived. William wouldn't have. Ivan was already making plans to send him to boarding school. Which meant he would be raised by strangers. I couldn't let that happen.'' She looked down at her hands. Then back up at him. "I couldn't.''

"So you called me.''

"I called you.'' Just as pride hadn't been able to stop her from contacting this man she still loved but couldn't have, pride couldn't stop her from saving William. And to save him from a man whose only motives for marriage were power and greed, she'd swallowed that pride and turned to Gregory for the strength she'd known he would offer.

"And what do you want from me now? Just what do you expect from me?''

"I expect that you will be the man I know you to be. I've seen you with William. I've watched you fall in love with him even before you knew he was yours. And I've seen him come alive under your loving hand.''

He looked away. Looked defeated.

"I've had to make choices, Gregory. From where you stand, they may not have been wise ones. They may not have been the right ones. But you weren't standing where I was. You weren't there—''

"I wasn't given the chance to be there!'' he ground out, his voice as raw as the look in his eyes.

She accepted then that it was well and truly over. He would not understand. And from his perspective, Anna conceded that he could not understand.

"I have to go back,'' she said in a voice so quiet, she wasn't sure, at first, if he'd heard her. "I have to go back,'' she repeated as he met her eyes with a look of utter incredulity.

"To what? The loving arms of your family?'' He

snorted in disgust. "For what? A crumbling little country that nothing short of a miracle or an arranged marriage can save? Help me understand this."

She drew herself erect. "I am a princess," she said simply. "I have a responsibility. I have a duty."

The rage in his eyes outdistanced even his disbelief. "They browbeat you, they threaten you—they barter you, for God sake, like a piece of property, like an object, like a possession whose only worth can be measured in dollars—and yet you go back to them."

"I don't expect you to understand."

He stared at her hard, gathered his composure, lost it in the same breath. "You're damn right I don't understand. But you need to understand something. You will not…" he paused, slammed his fist on the table, visibly steadied himself. "You will not take him away from me."

She felt as if she was bleeding. She felt as if she was dying as she met his eyes levelly, utterly defeated yet totally committed to do what was best for William. "No. I won't take him away from you."

Ten

Anna had come full circle. Once again, she was aboard Langley's private jet. And once again, she had left by cover of night, this time to escape the unwanted attention of the press that continued to hound Casa Royale. The major difference between this flight and the last, however, was that this time, the course had been set to take her back to Obersbourg. After several solitary hours, she was almost home.

Home. Yes, she was almost home, yet everything inside her said it was home she had left behind in Texas.

As she felt the aircraft's gradual descent, which heralded the approach to the airport, she could still see the troubled looks on the faces in the small crowd that had gathered to see her off. Blake and Josie had come. So had the Churchills, the Cunninghams, the Langleys. Even Manny and Sheila had come to say goodbye, smiling sadly. But it was the remote distance in Gregory's eyes that haunted her. The confusion in William's that clutched at her heart and twisted.

"We'll see each other again, soon," she had promised William, forcing a lightness in her tone for his benefit. "Momma has some business to take care of with Grandfather and Grandmother. Gregory will take good care of you. You'll get to ride Bea. And play with Tito and Cosmo. I'll call you every day, and you can tell me about everything you've done."

They hadn't told William that Gregory was his father. The time was not yet right. Neither had they talked about when she would return, if she would return, how they would share their child. She only knew she couldn't bear to deprive William of his father any longer—just like she knew she couldn't live without William forever, either.

Her decision to leave so abruptly had been prompted by Gregory's actions. She had done what she could do to make amends, but her duplicity had fostered the return of his cold, distant disdain. She accepted and understood his reaction. Had been prepared for the loss of his love.

But not for the pain. She'd known then that there was nothing to keep her in Texas. Nothing but Gregory, who she loved more than life, the twins, who she loved like her own, and her son, her beautiful precious child, who she could no longer deprive of his father and the chance to have the kind of normal life she and Sara had never known.

In resigned silence, she stared out the window as the coastal seaport of Obersbourg, hugged by the blue-green water of the Mediterranean, came into view. The knots in her stomach clenched into tight balls of dread at the prospect of facing her parents. Yet she'd made her choice—if it could be called a choice. No one could understand—especially Gregory—the ties that bound her to her country. No one could understand the inescapable fact of her heritage. Obersbourg was her obligation. Its people, her responsibility. Just as William's happiness was her responsibility.

She would do it again. No matter how badly it hurt, she would sacrifice everything to insure he experienced this chance at normalcy. Even though her heart had broken when she'd left him. She would not subject William to her parents' rule again. She would not allow the vivacious, precocious four-year-old she had always longed for him to be, turn back into a shadowy shell of a child.

The jet shuddered slightly as the landing gear dropped into place. She stared, unseeing, at the palace turrets lording above the city, refused to consider that she'd had any choice but to return. A return that had cost her everything.

Two words ran repeatedly through her mind as the earth seemed to reach up and meet the sky as the jet dropped, leveled, then kissed the runway in a smooth, effortless landing. *Love* and *duty*. It all came down to those two ultimate tests.

All that she loved, she had left behind in Texas.

All that was duty, she faced when she set foot on the tarmac in Obersbourg.

She unbuckled her seat belt, gathered her composure, and rose to her feet.

The first person she saw upon arrival at the palace was Royce. Her kind, faithful butler, Royce. She'd missed him. Missed only him, she acknowledged, and felt a small flicker of warmth trickle into a heart that had felt like ice since she'd left Texas behind.

As the limo door swung open and she approached the

grand staircase of the ornate but slightly tarnished splendor of the palace, Royce was the one person she was glad to see. Not her cold, uncaring parents, not her designer clothes and heirloom jewels, not the cars, the glamour, her personal chef, but her butler. Not because he was her servant, but because he was her friend. He knew and understood all that she and Sara had endured.

Royce was the son of a baker who had visited the palace as a little boy and decided it was where he wanted to live. That had been almost fifty years ago. And during his years of service, he'd been more parent to her than servant, more friend than subject. It had been Royce who had kissed her boo-boos when she was a child starved for affection, Royce who had stayed with her, holding her hand during the solitary ordeal of William's difficult delivery. And it had been Royce who had secreted his cell phone into her quarters and made it possible for her to call Gregory without the fear of the call being traced.

She could see by the soft smile on his face that, if necessary, Royce was ready to hold her hand again now. She hugged him hard and, with a look, let him know that this battle was hers and hers alone to fight.

"It's splendid to see you again, Miss," he said in his soft, polite way that expressed so much more than he deemed proper for someone in his position to verbalize.

"I've missed you," she confessed, holding his hands in hers. "And how is the climate in the palace these days?"

"Frigid," he answered with a sober look.

"In other words, business as usual." She forced a smile to reassure him. "It'll be all right. I can handle them. I'm ready to handle them," she added, seeing by the considering look in his eyes that he believed her.

"King Richard and Queen Caroline are waiting for you in the library."

Anna checked her watch. It was 3:00 p.m. "I assume dinner is still served at eight."

He nodded.

"Please extend my regrets to mother and father, but I won't be meeting with them until then. I want to rest and freshen up a bit first."

"They requested that I escort you directly to the library upon your arrival," he added with reluctance.

She smiled. "I'm sure it was more of a command than a request but, in any event, I'll meet with them at dinner. Express my regrets, will you please, Royce?"

Reading the determination in her eyes, sensing her newfound sense of confidence, Royce smiled, delighted with her blatant act of rebellion. "It will be my pleasure, Miss."

King Richard and Queen Caroline were quietly seething when Anna entered the family dining room at precisely 8:00 p.m. She hadn't realized how well she could read them until this very moment, when faced with their silent wrath.

They appeared rattled and angry, and to have given in to such raw, uncivilized emotions was, in their opinion, entirely unacceptable behavior for blooded aristocracy. This unexpected insight bolstered the confidence that had been flagging since Anna had made some key phone calls not fifteen minutes ago. Instead of cowing her, her father's barely controlled rage and her mother's empty stare only served to strengthen her resolve, lend support for the confrontation to come.

She sat down without a welcome. Ate without a word, taking note of an underlying fragility veiled behind her mother's blank eyes, discovering what she had never before dared to notice. Age had touched her invincible father, although not unkindly. His face, though lined, was still coldly handsome; the gray in his hair, much more than a trace, lent a subtle elegance that he wore as an inalienable right rather than the inevitable mark of time.

There was no sign that they were happy to see her. Of course, she'd expected none. What she'd expected was exactly what she was getting—their chilled silence, at least until the final course was served and finished. Then, and only then, would she be taken to task for her myriad transgressions.

What they expected from her, was capitulation. Complete and total. Knowing that they were about to have the priceless Persian rug pulled out from under them when she gave them anything but, added strength to her convictions, fostered a newfound confidence that rode on a fledgling rush of power.

"Mother, Father," she said, addressing them in a voice made strong by commitment, "we have many issues to discuss concerning the future of Obersbourg."

Two stunned faces acknowledged her insolence with glacial glares. Her mother's face drained to pale. Her father's mottled with his rising blood pressure.

"You dare to assume," the King accused, his voice carefully modulated to mask an unprecedented loss of control, "that I would entertain any discussion you would deem to initiate?"

"What I dare," she assured him, her gaze locked and steady on his, "is to assume my rightful place as my country's princess. What I dare to assume," she continued, as her father's combative stare attempted and failed to bring her to her knees, "is that your antiquated economic theories and failing commerce practices are robbing our country of the prosperity its people deserve.''

''How dare you!'' he demanded as he rose from the table, tossing aside his linen napkin with an exaggerated flourish.

''I dare,'' she countered, rising to her feet to equalize instead of diminish her power, ''because this is my birthright. I dare, because I am of royal blood and because I refuse to stand by one moment longer and watch our sovereignty slip away.''

''You are responsible for that!'' he roared, his face vivid red with rage. ''Because of you, Ivan is dead. There will be no marriage, no merging of power. Because of you, Obersbourg is hanging on the precipice of destruction. A seven-hundred-year-old dynasty is facing an end.''

''Ivan is dead because he was a coward. Seven hundred years ago, an arranged marriage may have been the only answer. Today we need to look toward untapped opportunities, not archaic rituals where fathers offer their daughters as prizes to the highest bidder.''

His hard eyes bored into hers. ''You, my dear daughter, are no prize.''

Cave-cold silence echoed off the damask paneled walls.

She'd thought she was immune to the special kind of pain he could administer. She was wrong. But she was not about to let it stop her.

''And you,'' she said, her every word laced with regret for everything that he'd never been, for everything she had ever wanted him to be, ''are a man without vision, a man without heart. To recover, Obersbourg needs both.''

"I suppose you think you are the one who will deliver."

"I will, absolutely, deliver. Starting tomorrow. I've called a cabinet meeting for 9:00 a.m. You may attend if you choose, but I will expect either your silence or your support."

Before the King could recover, she went on. "Do not force me to end your rule in disgrace. I would not want to have you declared mentally unfit to govern.

"And do not underestimate me, Father," she added when his shocked expression relayed he had reeled past disbelief. "I am not the browbeaten puppet who ran from you in fear last August. I returned to Obersbourg because I intend to offer our people the leadership they deserve. Do not doubt my motives or my determination. I will accomplish what I set out to do with or without your support. With or without your support," she repeated purposefully. "And never forget that I learned how to be ruthless from a master."

Neither her mother nor her father appeared capable of speech. She shook her head sadly, turned to leave the room, then stopped long enough to look back over her shoulder.

"You could have been so much more to me. To Sara and our children. We needed so much more from you. And now, it's too late. What compassion I have left, is reserved for my people. Do not make the mistake of doubting that, either."

Greg scanned an incoming fax, tossed it aside, then rose from his desk to stare grimly out the window. During the last month, he'd moved the bulk of his Pine Valley office to Casa Royale. It hadn't been that much of a transition. His small office at the ranch was already equipped with computer and fax. All he'd needed was the addition of his files, a few extra phone lines, a scanner and copier and he was in business. He had excellent staff manning Hunt Industries, kept in constant communication with them and was gradually shifting control of several projects into the capable hands of his project managers.

The relocation was a necessary adjustment on his part to ensure that William felt a sense of security. A sense of home.

From the window, he could see William and Tito and the ever patient Cosmo, engineering a sprawling network of highways in the huge sandpile he'd recently constructed at the edge of the garden.

God, how he loved the boy. Loved watching him. Loved discovering how his mind worked. He was a small miracle, an immense source of wonder and pride. That he could have been a part of making such an astonishing source of energy and intelligence was a constant source of amazement to him. That he had missed so much—four years—was a niggling and infuriating source of frustration that fueled an anger and fed a sense of betrayal that had corroded his feelings for Anna beyond recognition.

Restless, he walked back to his desk, even though his concentration was shot. He wasn't counting days, he told himself as his gaze darted to a desk calendar framed in brushed chrome. He wasn't consciously tallying the forty-two days and nights since Anna had flown out of his life and back to the one that had claimed both her allegiance and her presence.

"Juanita told me I'd find you here. Brooding."

He looked up at the sound of Blake's voice, crossed

his arms over his chest and leaned back in his leather chair.

Blake, Josie and the twins had arrived yesterday for an impromptu visit. To meddle, he suspected, on the pretense of worrying about how he was getting along with William. How he was getting along without Anna.

"I'm not brooding. I'm working. Some of us have obligations."

"And some of us recognize denial when we see it."

He shot Blake a stony glare—which only prompted a chuckle.

"What do you want, little brother?"

Blake hitched a hip on the corner of Greg's polished mahogany desk. "Just thought I'd catch you up on a little overseas activity—strictly a business update."

"Since when have you been interested in international finance?"

"Oh, since a certain princess appeared on the scene and set the European business world on its heels."

Greg didn't try to deny that he knew exactly what Blake was talking about. It was his business to keep abreast of any opportunities that Hunt Industries could take advantage of, both domestic and abroad. Under other circumstances he would have been jumping into the thick of the action in Obersbourg like a hockey player diving into a fight.

"You see this yet?" Blake asked casually as he tossed the latest copy of *Newsweek* onto the desk.

He'd seen it. Schooled himself to ignore it now. Yet he knew every detail of the cover photo.

A Portrait Of A Princess was printed in bold black letters beneath a recent photograph of Princess Anna von Oberland: beautiful, sedate, regal. She sat stiffly on Obersbourg's royal throne, a diamond-and-ruby tiara

atop her golden hair, heirloom jewels glittering at her
throat, dripping like tears from her ears. There was a
hollow, haunted look about the emerald eyes that met
the camera, a stark determination that even the reserved
warmth of a smile that held no joy couldn't conceal.

"In case you missed the article," Blake went on,
snagging the magazine and thumbing through it until he
found the page he'd marked, "I'll fill you in."

Greg pressed steepled fingers to his chin, knowing
there was nothing to do but wait Blake out.

"Here is it," he said, and began to read.

"The small principality of Obersbourg, nestled in
a picturesque elbow of the Mediterranean and all
but obscure for the past seven centuries, has made
news this past month when its princess, Anna von
Oberland, set the business world on the edge of its
collective seats. After seven hundred years of male-
dominated rule, the first woman in the history of
this tiny country of approximately twenty-five thousand subjects has taken over the reins of power.

"In an effort to regain her country's solvency—
and in the process avoid its loss of sovereignty to
France—the princess has initiated bold and daring
business ventures, offering as collateral a treasure
trove of heirloom jewels—many of which the princess is wearing in the cover photo—to finance a
massive refurbishing of the palace and converting
the first two stories into an exclusive gaming casino
that, it's rumored, will reduce Monaco's famed
gambling establishment to the equivalent of a
thatched hut."

Blake droned on. Greg shut him out. He didn't need
to hear any more. He practically knew the rest of the

article word for word. He'd read it several times, picturing the reporter's graphic description of Obersbourg—picturesque seaport city…breathtaking view of the Mediterranean…oldest ruling family in Europe…the palace's exquisite gardens, magnificent flowers, private zoo…destined to become the elite haunt of the world's rich and famous.

"Hocked the family jewels. Can you believe it?" Blake interjected with a chuckle. "The girl's got guts, I'll give her that—she set aside a pride that had kept her country wallowing toward financial ruin for centuries. She's got a damn good head for business, too, if you ask me."

"I don't recall asking."

Blake went on as if he hadn't heard Greg's dry comment. "She's opening up bids for a major aircraft plant to be located on the edge of the city, in another attempt to boost the failing economy. Seems to me we should be getting in on a piece of that action."

Greg arched a brow. "We?"

Blake had the good sense to look sheepish. "I'm a family man now. I figure maybe it's time I start taking an interest in the family business."

Greg snorted. "So now you're an instant expert."

"You're the expert. When you don't have your head up your—"

"What's going on in here?" Josie poked her head in the door, puzzled to see Blake grinning amiably into Greg's dark scowl.

"Just a little business discussion, darlin'," Blake said, snagging her arm and pulling her to his side.

"Oh, please. Sweetie, what you know about business

you could tuck into a button hole and have room left over for a Mercedes.''

This brought a grinning snort from Greg and a wounded look from Blake.

''So much for the cherish part of the vows,'' he said with a staged pout.

She wrapped her arms around his neck, pecked him lightly on the lips. ''Darling—you know there are other aspects of your sterling character that I highly cherish.''

Blake's grin spread wide. ''Oh, yeah. Just last night, you were cherishing the hell out of—''

She clamped a hand over his mouth, shot a bright, blinking smile Greg's way. ''We'll be getting out of your hair now.''

And with Blake tossing a wink over his shoulder, she led him out the door.

In grim silence, Greg watched them go. Happy for Blake—for what he'd found with Josie. Green with envy—and not much liking himself for it. He could have had that. He almost had. With Anna. Anna and William.

What he had now was William. And his pride. His damnable, stubborn pride.

Eleven

No one ever bothered Anna unannounced in her private office. Her mother never made an appearance, so when Royce rapped subtly on the door at 7:00 p.m., then opened it and announced that Queen Caroline wished to have a word with her, Anna could only stare in stunned silence as her mother stepped inside the room.

For a long moment, they stayed as they were, Anna assessing from behind her massive desk, her mother looking tentative and ill at ease.

''Yes? Was there something you wanted?'' she finally asked, maintaining a cool reserve that she had perfected to an art over the past month and a half.

With reservations, her mother moved to stand before Anna's desk. She averted her gaze from Anna's to sweep the array of papers, the soft hum of an incoming fax, the cursor blinking softly but steadily from the notebook computer that lay open on the devastatingly well-organized surface of the desk.

"What is it, Mother? I have several hours of work yet to complete tonight."

"You work too hard," her mother stated, meeting Anna's gaze at last.

Anna was stunned. Then suspiciously amused. "Your concern is misplaced—and far too late."

She hated the hard, cynical edge that had become a part of her manner. And for some reason, she hated even more the wince of pain that fleetingly crossed her mother's aristocratic features.

"My transgressions are many," Queen Caroline stated, squaring her shoulders. "As are my weaknesses."

She was quiet for a very long time as Anna searched her face and saw the sincere regret no longer masked behind a facade of indifference. "You are making a grave mistake, Anna."

Sensing, at last, what this meeting was about, Anna leaned back in her chair. "While usurping Father's power may have been ruthless, I do not see it as a mistake."

"I'm not talking about your father. While he fumes, I think he is silently relieved that he is no longer under the pressure of ruling Obersbourg. I'm talking about William."

Had she knocked her to the ground, Anna couldn't have felt less off balance. Or more angry. "William? When has my son, your grandson, ever been more than an inconvenient thought to you?"

While she did not blanch, a flicker of something very near to regret flashed in Caroline's eyes. "You have every right to be incensed. What you do not have a right to do, is judge me.''

"As I have been judged by you all my life?" Anna shot back bitterly.

Queen Caroline met her daughter's eyes squarely. "I have given up much for the sake of tradition. I have lost much for the sake of providence, for the sake of protocol in the guise of privilege.''

Intrigued, in spite of her resolve not to let the heavy remorse in her mother's voice phase her, Anna held her gaze. "What are you talking about?''

"I, too, was once in love," she confessed after a moment's hesitation and with such wistful hopelessness that Anna involuntarily leaned toward her. ''With—with a rebel and a rogue,'' she continued, the slight smile that lit her face telling of memories of a young love lost, a young life compromised.

"He was beneath me. In position. In everything that mattered to my family. They took me away from him. They arranged my marriage to your father. It was the accepted protocol. It was the…the established method of procreation of royal bloodlines.''

She looked quickly away from Anna's stunned gaze, but not before Anna saw the thin mist of moisture glistening in her gray-green eyes. "I was given no choice. And yet…and yet I've always regretted that I didn't…that I didn't at least attempt to run away. To run to him. As you ran to your young man.''

She clasped her hands together, as if that fragile hold would prevent her from falling apart. "I haven't shown it, Anna. But I have…I have admired your small rebellions.''

"Like you admired Sara's?" Anna couldn't stop the question. Couldn't deny herself the opportunity to level the kind of pain she sensed her mother was vulnerable to for the first time.

Regret, however, for her cruelty was swift and humbling. "I'm sorry. That was uncalled for."

"It was deserved," her mother replied, drawing from years of practiced control to move beyond the pain. "I was not what I could have been—not what I should have been for Sara, or for you. I cannot rectify that horrific error. I cannot justify. I can only ask you to consider that my heart closed the day they took me away from…from him…and forced me to marry your father."

She drew on her reserves to square her shoulders, lift her chin. "Do not become him, Anna. Do not allow everything that is you—your kindness, your giving heart, your ability to love and be loved. Do not allow yourself to be lost in a void of your father's making."

Tears stung Anna's eyes, clogged her throat as her mother laid herself bare, laid out a picture of the woman Anna feared she had already become.

"Why now?" she demanded rising to her feet, her hands fisted to her sides to keep them steady. "I've needed you for so long. Why do you come to me now?"

Queen Caroline closed her eyes, fought back tears both she and her daughter had thought she was incapable of shedding. "Because now," she managed, facing Anna's confusion and pain, "now is the time that matters most."

"I don't understand."

Caroline walked slowly to the door. "You will. You have loved, Anna. You still love."

"What love I had is lost."

Her mother turned, met her eyes with a wistful smile. "There is someone here to see you, my dear. Please try to consider my words when you make your peace with him.''

She opened the door then, opened it wide—to allow Gregory to step inside.

Greg wasn't entirely prepared for what he would say. He'd only known that a part of him had been lost since the day he'd let Anna walk out of his life. Seeing her now—her eyes full of shock, valiantly hiding a hope, fruitlessly masking a hurt—made him realize that seeing her again filled a hole the size of Texas that had been drilled through the middle of his heart.

Finding an unexpected ally in the Queen herself had been a stroke of luck he hadn't counted on. He'd been prepared to scale the palace walls if necessary. He'd done it before, under cover of dark, under the auspices of heroism. He'd have done it today for love. He'd have done it today out of desperation.

She opened her mouth as if to speak—then quickly whirled away from him, presenting her back, wrapping her arms around her waist as if stalling a chill that had suddenly come over her like an arctic wind.

''Your Highness,'' he said, an acknowledgment, an address that brought her head around. ''You look like hell.''

His thin smile was intended to soften the harshness of the words his concern had not adequately relayed.

''William,'' she said without acknowledging any of the emotions roiling inside her. ''Where is William? Is he all right?''

''He's fine. He's here. Whoa. Not so fast.'' He stopped her with a gentle but firm hand on her arm as she shot for the door. ''He's in the kitchen—don't ask me which one. He's with your butler eating cookies. Your mother poured the milk.''

"I want to see him."

No match for his grip on her arm, she was forced to stop, glare up at him.

"And you will. You will see him," he assured her with a patience he didn't know he had in him. "We need to talk, Anna. First we need to talk."

She was edgy. She was alert—for Lord knew what, he thought—and he reined in his temper when he looked, really looked deep into her eyes.

In spite of the beauty of the face he had dreamed about every night since he'd let her walk away from him, the strain of the schedule she'd been keeping, the pressure to perform and the burden of responsibility had taken their toll. Her expressive mouth was pinched and drawn. Those clear green eyes looked fogged from stress and lack of sleep.

"Sit, Anna. Please sit and talk with me."

"I wasn't aware that there was anything you wanted to hear me say," she said, reluctantly capitulating by sitting stiffly on a damask side chair.

"Did I ever tell you," he began as he pulled a matching chair around to face her, to lean forward and take her cold, fragile hands in his, "did I ever tell you that I can be a thickheaded fool if adequately provoked?"

She looked from their joined hands to his eyes, back to his hands again, but not before he'd caught the quick, telling shadow of hope. It was all the opening he needed.

"I wanted to hate you, Anna, for what you'd done. What you'd denied me." Eyes on her lowered head, he watched her swallow, held on tight when she tried to pull her hands from his grip. "I couldn't. I couldn't hate you—the problem was, everyone knew it but me. Juanita drove me crazy. Blake—Blake does not yet know how close he came to having that ugly mug of his rearranged. More than once,'' he added with a rueful grin.

The only acknowledgment that she was listening was a small easing of tension in the hands he held.

"Every night when you called William,'' he went on, needing to get the words out, "it hurt. It hurt that you didn't ask to speak to me. It hurt that you were functioning so well, when I was—well, let's just say when I wasn't functioning at all.''

Her head came up at that, and that small glimmer of hope had transitioned to a studied curiosity.

"After you left Texas, left your child—our child—the child that you loved more than life, I began to think back to some of the things you had said. Some of the things you didn't say. I made myself take the time to rethink them.

"What I couldn't understand was how you could be willing to give up everything—William, me—for your noble obligations—''

"You were not mine to give up,'' she insisted. "You made it clear—you didn't want me there.''

"I was angry. I'm still angry,'' he confessed. "I'm angry for the time I lost with William. I'm angry for the time I lost with you. I'm angry, but no longer at you. It took a while, but I finally understand what compelled you. I understand what drove you.''

He shifted, leaning closer. "It's not anything as simple as duty, is it? It's not anything as basic as obligation. It's your heart, Anna. It's that honorable, incorruptible heart that makes you always take responsibility, take the blame, take on the task of setting a world full of wrongs right.''

He let his words, which had been so long forming in

his mind, settle before he went down on one knee in front of her.

"I finally realized that it wasn't a cold, calculating woman who could convince a young marine she didn't love him in order to save him from a lifestyle she was afraid would smother him. It wasn't a designing woman who could give up flesh and blood so they could have a chance at a life that would enable instead of disable them. And it wasn't a selfish, aristocratic snob who would leave a simple life she'd grown to love, a country she had embraced, to return to a dying principality and try to save it from ruin.

"What you are, Anna," he continued, bringing her hands to his mouth and pressing a soft kiss there, "is a proud and valiant woman who has taken more upon her slim shoulders than any one person should have to take."

The warmth of her tears fell softly on their joined hands. He stood. Drew her up with him. Into his arms. Breathed a huge sigh of relief when she melted against him like warm honey.

"I let you down," he whispered against her hair. "I sold you short. I ignored your love, stepped on your heart, took away your child. Can you ever forgive me?"

In answer, she wrapped her arms tighter around his neck and hung on. Just hung on.

Later, after she and William had enjoyed a tearful, sloppy, reunion, and Royce had fed them both, Anna and Greg tucked their son into bed in the room adjoining her suite.

Not long after, Greg had her naked and snug by his side under satin sheets and an antique lace counterpane. He glanced from the towering spires of the four-poster, the gilded, ornate molding that adorned the twenty foot high walls, the silk brocade wallpaper and the Louis the XIV dresser and side chairs.

"It ain't much, but it's home," he said after a long, appreciative whistle.

She smiled against his shoulder, wove her fingers through his chest hair. "Texas is home."

"Yes," he agreed. "And one of the advantages of owning my own aircraft plant will factor in just fine. We're all going to log a lot of air time scooting between here and Royal for, oh, say, the next sixty or seventy years."

"You would do that? Commute long distance for me? What about your work?"

"An offshoot of all this soul-searching is that I've found I have very capable people who can handle several aspects of the business for me. In time, once you have everything set in motion here, you'll need to select some key people you trust to run the show for you while you're stateside."

"With the Web, phone and fax, I'm planning on stateside being a major part of my life."

"You miss the garden."

"I miss the garden."

"You know," he said, hitching up on an elbow so he could look down into her precious, trusting face, "when I was trying to come to terms with who you are and why you did what you did, I'd find myself sitting on that bench by the fountain that had fascinated you so."

Lazily, he toyed with a strand of her hair. "I think I know now why it had always drawn you. You saw parallels there. You saw yourself in the transplanted vegetation, saw that with determination, will and careful nurturing, even life alien to the rugged Texas terrain could thrive.

"You saw Will making the transition. What you didn't see was yourself."

He lowered his head to brush a kiss across her brow. "I'll always see you there, Anna. I see you thriving. I see a delicate balance between your role as a princess and your role as my wife."

"If that was a proposal," she murmured, pulling his mouth to hers, "I accept."

"It was definitely a proposal. And I wouldn't have taken no for an answer."

"How do you feel about big weddings?"

He looked deeply into those eyes he loved, knowing, as he did, that there was more to her question than a mere question. "Big weddings?"

"I'm thinking extravaganza. I'm thinking the fairy-tale wedding of the century between Europe's most photographed princess and the Lone Star state's most photogenic prince."

His eyes narrowed in appreciation. "You're thinking revenue."

"Oh, am I. The press has capitalized from royalty for years. It's time for me to take advantage of them. Can you imagine the tourist dollars a highly publicized wedding could bring to Obersbourg?"

He smiled.

"You don't mind?"

"What? That you want exploit the expression of my undying love by making it into a media circus? All for the sake of helping bail out Obersbourg's economy?"

"That pretty well sums it up."

"Well, darling, let me sum up my admiration for your business savvy this way."

He kissed her then. Long, deep, lovingly. "Go for it. But we have the real wedding back in Royal. At the Cattleman's Club."

"Deal," she said and kissed him again—then struggled abruptly to get up. "Oh, my. Let me up. I forgot. I have a critical conference call scheduled in ten minutes."

Lazily he watched her slip out of bed, appreciating the view, anticipating the night to come. "Conference call with who?"

"With the head of Avalon Air. We're about to go to contract with them."

"The contract for the aircraft plant? The one that will rocket Obersbourg's employment rate into the ninety plus percent? The one that's going to pad the royal coffers with approximately—" he paused, then stated the precise figure as he plumped his pillow and crossed his hands behind his head.

A pale-blue silk robe clutched to her breasts, she turned abruptly. "How did you know the exact figure?"

"A little bird told me?"

She crossed slowly back to the bed, her brows narrowed. "What do you know about Avalon Air?"

He stared thoughtfully at the ceiling. "Oh, I know it's an up-and-coming corporation. A subsidiary of a major player in the aviation industry."

"Subsidiary of what major player?" she asked pointedly.

"Hunt Industries," he said with a grin.

"You—you're the owner of Avalon Air?"

"Well, actually, yeah."

He dodged the pillow she swung at him.

"What was that for?"

"For bailing me out behind my back, when it was important for me to—"

He snagged her wrist, pulled her down to the bed, dragged her beneath him. "When it was important for you to do this by yourself. Well I hate to let all this red-hot temper go to waste," he said with a grin as he nuzzled her throat, "but you did do it by yourself."

When she made a huff of disgust, he defended himself. "Hey, it's a hell of an opportunity. I had to scramble like crazy to get up to snuff on the specs, then compile a bid that would outshoot the other guns and guarantee Hunt Industries a tidy profit. And yes," he added before she could voice another protest, "I would have been in on this sweet deal even if you weren't the one offering it up."

"It's a question of free enterprise, then."

"Profit margins," he countered with a grin so wicked it finally earned her smile.

"Are you going to make love to me?" she asked as she shifted beneath him, taking his weight, returning his kiss, welcoming him to the home they had found in each other's arms.

"Oh, I'm going to make love to you, all right," he promised, loving the feel of her beneath him as much as he loved the smile that had been so achingly absent in his life.

Epilogue

It was the media event of the century. Not since Prince Rainier and Princess Grace's public and spectacular wedding four decades ago, had the world witnessed such a fairy-tale extravaganza. And not since Princess Diana had the world fallen so deeply in love with the princess who had risked all to ensure security for her people.

It was a glorious spring day—so ordered by royal decree. Hundreds of thousands of tourists had flooded the tiny principality hoping to catch a glimpse of the royal couple, to in some small way be a part of such a historic event.

Flag-flying yachts littered the picturesque harbor of the Mediterranean seaport capital, flowers floated in festive celebration on the water, fireworks erupted like jewels at midnight. The princess bride, adorned in acres of trailing satin and antique lace, walked down a silk-paved aisle toward her handsome and newly knighted American upstart, sharing her love, sharing their day with the world watching on.

"You're looking very beautiful—and very smug," Greg observed three weeks later as he twirled Anna around the ballroom of the Texas Cattleman's Club.

Not an hour ago, they had renewed their vows, Texas style, in the grand salon of the Club, with Greg's family and their friends looking on. In actuality, it seemed to Anna that half of West Texas had shown up for a lavish reception for the newlyweds, who had recently returned to Royal and an extended honeymoon at Casa Royale.

"I'm feeling very smug," she said, as he twirled her past a vivacious Harriet, who was currently charming the starch from Royce's very staid and reserved smile.

"Because you pulled it off? Because you've managed, almost single-handedly, to snatch Obersbourg from the jaws of a financial crisis? Because now that we're married, William is the legitimate male heir to the throne, which ends the final threat of loss of sovereignty?" The heir in question grinned at his mother from across the room as he and Tito dove into two huge pieces of snowy-white wedding cake.

"You've been reading too many magazine articles." Her bright eyes danced from her son to her husband. "It makes me sound very mercenary."

"Mercenary? No. Intelligent, savvy—sexy," he added on a low growl as he pressed his lips to her ear. "I can't wait to get you alone."

"Was it destiny, do you think?" she asked, caressing his nape, pulling back to look deeply into his eyes. "That we found each other, that we made our beautiful son together, that nothing and no one was able to keep us apart?"

"Destiny. Fate. Kismet. Whatever it was, it was meant to be."

They stopped, as one, eyes only for each other as he drew her into a sweet, sealing kiss. "I love you, Anna."

"And I love you. For so many reasons. But most of all, for making me believe again—in fairy tales. In happily ever after."

Hank Langley, Forrest Cunningham, Sterling Churchill, and Blake observed the happy couple from their roosts at the edge of the dance floor.

"Kind of makes your heart go pitty-pat, seeing all that wedded bliss," Hank observed with a grin.

Beside him, Forrest hooked a thumb into the pocket of his tuxedo trousers. "You realize, he's the last of the Alpha team to bite the dust."

Sterling chuckled. "Well, they always say there's strength in numbers."

"Who knew," Blake said thoughtfully, "that when we launched the mission last summer, we'd all end up married within nine months."

"It was a rush, wasn't it?" Forrest segued, darting a glance from one man to the next. "The danger. The excitement of stealing a princess out from under the royal guard?"

Sterling drained his glass of champagne. "Yeah. Makes you wonder, with our composite skills and connections, what else we'd be capable of pulling off if the need arose."

"Well, I know one thing," Hank put in, returning the smile Callie sent him from across the room. "The Club's membership is littered with forceful, wealthy and daring men. Count them in and count me out of any further activities."

"My covert mission days are over, too," Blake said

with conviction. "I'd say it's a pretty safe bet that Greg's are, too. That's one contented man if ever I've seen one."

In companionable silence, the four men watched the bride and groom sway, as one, to the rhythm of the wedding waltz. Of the same mind, their gazes sought and found their own wives, as they quite happily acknowledged that they had all the excitement they would ever need in their ladies' loving arms.

* * * * *

LINDSAY McKENNA
continues her heart-stopping series:

MORGAN'S MERCENARIES
III
THE HUNTERS

Coming in October 1999:
HUNTER'S PRIDE
Special Edition #1274

Devlin Hunter had a way with the ladies, but when it came to his job as a mercenary, the brooding bachelor worked alone. Then his latest assignment paired him up with Kulani Dawson, a feisty beauty whose tender vulnerabilities brought out his every protective instinct—and chipped away at his proud vow never to fall in love....

Coming in January 2000:
THE UNTAMED HUNTER
Silhouette Desire #1262

Rock-solid Shep Hunter was unconquerable—until his mission brought him face-to-face with Dr. Maggie Harper, the woman who'd walked away from him years ago. Now Shep struggled to keep strong-willed Maggie under his command without giving up the steel-clad grip on his heart....

Look for Inca's story when Lindsay McKenna continues the MORGAN'S MERCENARIES series with a brand-new, longer-length single title—coming in 2000!

Available at your favorite retail outlet.

Silhouette®

If you enjoyed what you just read,
then we've got an offer you can't resist!

Take 2 bestselling
love stories FREE!
Plus get a FREE surprise gift!

Clip this page and mail it to Silhouette Reader Service™

IN U.S.A.	**IN CANADA**
3010 Walden Ave.	P.O. Box 609
P.O. Box 1867	Fort Erie, Ontario
Buffalo, N.Y. 14240-1867	L2A 5X3

YES! Please send me 2 free Silhouette Desire® novels and my free surprise gift. Then send me 6 brand-new novels every month, which I will receive months before they're available in stores. In the U.S.A., bill me at the bargain price of $3.12 plus 25¢ delivery per book and applicable sales tax, if any*. In Canada, bill me at the bargain price of $3.49 plus 25¢ delivery per book and applicable taxes**. That's the complete price and a savings of over 10% off the cover prices—what a great deal! I understand that accepting the 2 free books and gift places me under no obligation ever to buy any books. I can always return a shipment and cancel at any time. Even if I never buy another book from Silhouette, the 2 free books and gift are mine to keep forever. So why not take us up on our invitation. You'll be glad you did!

225 SEN CNFA
326 SEN CNFC

Name	(PLEASE PRINT)	
Address	Apt.#	
City	State/Prov.	Zip/Postal Code

* Terms and prices subject to change without notice. Sales tax applicable in N.Y.
** Canadian residents will be charged applicable provincial taxes and GST.
  All orders subject to approval. Offer limited to one per household.
  ® are registered trademarks of Harlequin Enterprises Limited.

DES99   ©1998 Harlequin Enterprises Limited

**Start celebrating Silhouette's 20th anniversary
with these 4 special titles by
New York Times bestselling authors**

Fire and Rain
by Elizabeth Lowell

King of the Castle
by Heather Graham Pozzessere

State Secrets
by Linda Lael Miller

Paint Me Rainbows
by Fern Michaels

On sale in December 1999

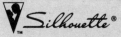

Celebrate Silhouette's 20th Anniversary

With beloved authors, exciting new miniseries and special keepsake collections, **plus** the chance to enter our 20th anniversary contest, in which one lucky reader wins the trip of a lifetime!

Take a look at who's celebrating with us:

DIANA PALMER
April 2000: SOLDIERS OF FORTUNE
May 2000 in Silhouette Romance: *Mercenary's Woman*

NORA ROBERTS
May 2000: IRISH HEARTS, the 2-in-1 keepsake collection
June 2000 in Special Edition: *Irish Rebel*

LINDA HOWARD
July 2000: MACKENZIE'S MISSION
August 2000 in Intimate Moments: *A Game of Chance*

ANNETTE BROADRICK
October 2000: a special keepsake collection, plus a brand-new title in
November 2000 in Desire

Available at your favorite retail outlet.

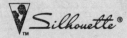

EXTRA! EXTRA!

The book all your favorite authors are raving about is finally here!

The 1999 Harlequin and Silhouette coupon book.

Each page is alive with savings that can't be beat!

Getting this incredible coupon book is as easy as 1, 2, 3.

1. During the months of November and December 1999 buy any 2 Harlequin or Silhouette books.

2. Send us your name, address and 2 proofs of purchase (cash receipt) to the address below.

3. Harlequin will send you a coupon book worth $10.00 off future purchases of Harlequin or Silhouette books in 2000.

Send us 3 cash register receipts as proofs of purchase and we will send you 2 coupon books worth a total saving of $20.00 (limit of 2 coupon books per customer).

Saving money has never been this easy.

Please allow 4-6 weeks for delivery. Offer expires December 31, 1999.

I accept your offer! Please send me (a) coupon booklet(s):

Name: _____

Address: _____ City: _____

State/Prov.: _____ Zip/Postal Code: _____

Send your name and address, along with your cash register receipts as proofs of purchase, to:

In the U.S.: Harlequin Books, P.O. Box 9057, Buffalo, N.Y. 14269

In Canada: Harlequin Books, P.O. Box 622, Fort Erie, Ontario L2A 5X3

Order your books and accept this coupon offer through our web site
http://www.romance.net

Valid in U.S. and Canada only.   PHQ4994R